The Annual Big Arsenic Fishing Contest!

Also by John Nichols

The Annual Big Arsenic Fishing Contest!

a novel

JOHN NICHOLS

University of New Mexico Press
Albuquerque

21 20 19 18 17 16   1 2 3 4 5 6

Library of Congress Cataloging-in-Publication Data

Names: Nichols, John Treadwell, 1940– author.
Title: The annual big arsenic fishing contest! : a novel /
John Nichols.
Description: First edition. | Albuquerque :
University of New Mexico Press, 2016.
Identifiers: LCCN 2016000667 (print) | LCCN 2016004868
(ebook) | ISBN 9780826357205 (hardcover : acid-free paper)
| ISBN 9780826357212 (electronic)
Classification: LCC PS3564.I274 A85 2016 (print)
| LCC PS3564.I274 (ebook) | DDC 813/.54—dc23
LC record available at http://lccn.loc.gov/2016000667

Cover illustrations courtesy of Dennis Haggerty
Author photo courtesy of Susan Crutchfield
Designed by Lila Sanchez
Composed in Warnock Pro and ITC Caslon 224 Std

To DOUG, MIKE, AND ME
We sure had fun.

Winning isn't everything, it's the only thing.

—*Vince Lombardi*

Friendship first, competition second.

—*Mao Tse-tung*

A Note to the Reader

This novel is a work of fiction based on the belief that "if you want to know the truth you've got to make it up." Any similarity between my characters and real people is coincidental. Fishing is inherently a game of liar's poker, and so is the allegory you are about to read.

One

For well over thirty years I have been enraptured by the Río Grande gorge and the river that runs through it up here in northern New Mexico only a few miles west of the Sangre de Cristo Mountains. Those mountains ramble along the eastern side of the wild county I have lived in since 1970, when I moved out west from New York City to save my soul, raise a family, and get right with the natural world.

From Ute Mountain, which lies close to the Colorado border, down to the picturesque apple town of Velarde, a distance of sixty-five miles, the Río Grande runs between dramatic and often sheer cliff walls. The cliffs are as modest as 100 feet high in some areas, yet rise to 650 feet where a bridge spanning the gorge (completed in 1968) has lately become the suicide capital of our impoverished state. Though we *norteños* inhabit unforgettable geography, our human socioeconomics stink. There's way too much heroin, way too few jobs, and class and racial tensions underlie every social interaction. That's not what I'm eager to talk about, however: I have other fish to fry.

. . .

My friends Yuri Stone and Bubba Baxter had about as much in common as Mickey Rooney and Joseph Stalin. Yuri was a half-pint (five foot three) second-generation Polish Jew my age who grew up in the Strawberry Mansion ghetto of Philadelphia and currently earned a living writing outdoor articles about fishing for *Sports Afield*, *Gray's Sporting Journal*, and *Bassmaster Magazine* (to name a few). Off the clock, early in the mornings before anyone else was awake, he crouched in a tiny cubicle in his Center City rent-control just off Rittenhouse Square surrounded by swirls of pipe smoke, revising a novel that he had been working on for many years. Yuri resembled a diminutive cartoon Italian gangster, yet he came from a literate family of card-carrying communists who had attended symphonies and the opera on weekends. Yuri himself had graduated second in his journalism class from Temple University, and he could also run fifty balls shooting straight cowboy pool. Despite being small, Yuri had a mouth louder than an evangelist's, and he was a serious intellectual. For the last twenty-five years he had been reading his way carefully through much of Western philosophy, from Thales, Socrates, and Plato to William James, Heidegger, and Sartre. Which was no small accomplishment for a hook-nosed lefty three pounds lighter than an old sponge, yet intensely aggressive. I recall once we were sitting in a Times Square automat scarfing macaroni and cheese when a beefy dweeb at the next table started flinging around the N-word with a careless lack of rectitude. Yuri didn't ask him to desist, already, he simply grabbed the ketchup bottle on our table and lunged at the guy, spewing obscenities as he swung for the rafters. You don't grow up in a jungle like Strawberry Mansion without carrying a big chip on your shoulder. What was Yuri's mantra a propos survival?

"Always throw the first punch."

My other friend, Bubba Baxter, was born and raised in Lubbock, Texas, by a family of born-agains who ate barbecue eight days a week and rarely met a vegetable they liked. Orville Baxter painted houses for a living, then he worked in a cotton operation, renovating their gins. Later, he was a skilled mechanic on big farm machinery; a guy who installed air conditioners and repaired them; and a maintenance foreman and janitor in the city schools. Salt of the earth. All Baxter family members believed in the Dallas Cowboys, and rooted for God (every Sunday during the season) to help the Cowboys win the Super Bowl. I wouldn't say Bubba was not smart, because he had actually graduated from Texas Tech with close to a 4.0 average as an English major, yet he exuded more than his fair share of genetic defects common to any resident of the Lone Star State. Though Bubba wasn't that big, only about five ten in his Tony Lamas, he even had muscles in his pug nose and was as fierce as a wolverine, having played starting noseguard for the Red Raiders when Jason Rafferty had been in charge of the defense some years before he defected to Hayden Fry at SMU, then squealed to the NCAA that subsequently murdered the Mustangs' football program.

In his heyday Bubba could bench press four hundred pounds, just ask him. He ran after women like a greyhound chasing mechanical rabbits at the dog track. Bubba had the good looks and the scoundrel charm of, say, Brad Pitt in the movie *Thelma and Louise,* and although his hustle was as transparent as a pane of glass, the ladies found him attractive anyway. Call him an archetypal Texas bounder . . . with lots of mendacious savvy. Just before you blew him off as a fanfaronading blockhead, Bubba could flick a switch and start conversing about Federal Reserve interest rates, voter registration fraud in the deep South, and Kurt Vonnegut's great novel, *Slaughterhouse-Five.* He could also be a bully whose idea of sophistical discourse was to shout you down with more megadecibels than a foghorn on a fancy ocean liner. Yet my friend had a cockeyed sense of humor that tickled me pink, and he was so full of energy and stark-raving chutzpah that it was fun to be with him. "Fun for the feeble minded," we kids used to say. And I suppose if the shoe fits, wear it.

I'm not saying *I'm* not obnoxious and noisy as well, nor am I insinuating that Yuri was not annoying and strident, either. Nobody likes a pot calling other kettles black. Still, Bubba Baxter could crank insufferable up to another level entirely. To make it worse, as the owner/operator of a chain of athletic spas called Racket Ranches located throughout the western United States, over the time we were friends Bubba became rich. He corralled the moola. Piles of leafy green. They say behind every fortune there's a great crime and I have no doubt that that was true in his case. Then again, against type, Bubba was very generous, at least to his friends. Once he had accumulated that gelt he always picked up the tab.

At all times Bubba had an expensive white Stetson cowboy hat settled rakishly atop his blond feathered locks (reminiscent of George Armstrong Custer or Brian Bosworth when he was a linebacker at Oklahoma), and around his waist he wore a two-gun holster set with a high-priced lawyer jammed into each holster. That's how Bubba conducted business: he sued *everybody*, and he usually won. "Bugger them before they bugger you," was his motto. It might just as well have been, "Always throw the first punch." Bubba would shout "Guns up!" and sic a lawyer on you faster than John Wayne used to be able to fast draw a Colt Dragoon cavalry pistol. It was just "bidness," nothing personal. Bubba could also double-talk you so effectively that you never understood what the hell he was driving at until it was too late. Texas bullshit grows on trees bigger than California Sequoias. That said, you had to admire the creative excess of his ribald gobbledygook. It was drop-dead hilarious.

• • •

To get right to it, the crux of my story is this: all three of us loved to fish. Yuri had been patronizing Atlantic-ocean party boats ever since he was knee-high to a pit bull. "When I was five I could sit in a rowboat all day long on Barnegat Bay with a bamboo pole and a bobbin feeding shiners to snapper blues." His pop had bought him a Zebco reel when he was six, teaching him how to use it on the banks of the Schuylkill River. After Yuri and I became friends he'd get me down on the Jersey shore when the stripers were running for all-night bouts on the beach using surf rods baited with eels to catch the monster sea bass. I personally never got the hang of it, failing to haul in anything even remotely large enough to legally keep. Yuri, however, regularly landed fish almost as large as himself. Chopping them up later was like butchering hogs in Upton Sinclair's Chicago stockyards. My friend handled a sharp knife like Zorro in a sword fight with the Count of Monte Cristo. Repeatedly he sharpened the blade on a damp whetstone the same way he incessantly chalked his cue tips in the pool halls. Though I was not crazy about coating myself up to the elbows in piscine blood and gore, Yuri loved it. He wrapped the filets in wax paper held shut with duct tape and distributed the packets to his homeboys in South Philly or up Strawberry Mansion way where he'd been raised in a neighborhood that was half-Jewish, half-black, with "a moderate garnishing of wops and Borinqueños." I enjoyed tagging after him during these deliveries. Yuri knew everybody on the street, in the barbershops and the pool halls, or even shining shoes outside a candy store whose display window was full of stale Milky Ways, empty Nehi orange pop bottles, and spider webs because it was only used as a drop-off for the Mafia. That's when I learned that most human beings who occupy inner-city America are named "Yo," "Hey, you," and "My man." Yuri produced the filets out of his cooler like Jesus—or more properly, Jesús—apportioning loaves and fishes. For me, these excursions to disseminate the ocean's bounty were like an adventure in Oz, a land I had never before visited. "This is my friend, the aristocrat," was Yuri's introduction of me to the brothers. I fumbled a lot trying to get the bro grip and knuckle bump greeting convolutions down pat with the corner boys and Mummer wannabes, even way back then. When we leaned against parked cars chowing down on Pat's cheese steaks or a hot Philadelphia pretzel slobbered in mustard, Yuri liked to ask me, "So whaddaya think of my town?" I always replied, "It has a nice aura, but it'll never be New York."

"I detest the Yankees," Yuri replied. "You want another? I'm paying. Your money's no good here."

These days he was more upscale. Yuri traveled around the lower United States, Newfoundland, Alaska, and Venezuela fishing for Arctic grayling, alligator gar in the Atchafalaya, and peacock bass on the Orinoco so that he could write about them for the hook and bullet journals that paid his expenses and ponied up generous kill fees to boot if they passed on his original stories.

Me, I also loved to fish, having finally learned, soon after I reached New Mexico in 1970, how to cast artificial flies at the feisty salmonids of our narrow mountain streams, especially the Río Chiquito, Pot Creek, and the Rito Sin Nombre where a "monster" might measure out at nine inches long. By 1979 I had graduated to the Nobodaddy of our area, the Río Grande, which runs from Creede high in the San Juan Mountains of Colorado down to the Gulf of Mexico. Much of the river in my county was inaccessible except for a few narrow paths, often nearly invisible, that zigzagged down the steep canyon walls. That stretch of Río Grande was not only chock-full of chubby fish but also a sensational state of mind, a rough-and-tumble paradise where you could still feel primal vestiges of Eden wriggling at the tip of your line.

Bubba himself had grown up ardently hunting and fishing in Texas, a style of sporting activity that I picture more akin to the atomic bomb on Hiroshima; there's nothing subtle about Texas. Still, the outdoors is the outdoors. In it, Bubba's dad, Orville, had had fun extirpating just about anything that gallivanted through a Texas swamp or a bayou rice paddy with whatever size weapon was available, preferably a big one. Around the Lubbock area about all you could shoot were boll weevils, so Orville Baxter was a traveling man. He and his boys, Bubba and the older brother, Brian, motored all over Texas in a Winnebago Brave passing many bucolic hours throughout wild nature looking to abrogate the longevity of its denizens. Brian's full name was Brian Benjamin Baxter, so in the beginning everybody wanted to call him B. B. The appellation never stuck, though, because Brian did not fit the nickname. He wasn't colorful. A tall, shy kid and retiring adult, he quit hunting at age nineteen for the simple reason that he hated killing things. Not so, Bubba. As an adult he loved to slaughter doves by the millions down near Edinburg, McAllen, and Harlingen so that his Mexican peones could pluck them. And he enjoyed "harvesting" redfish off of Galveston by tossing hand grenades overboard. Okay, I'm exaggerating, though not by a whole lot. If you mentioned "catch and release" to Bubba he would commence foaming at the mouth. "What are you talking about, you limp-wristed commie spear chucker, did your mother cut off your manhood or something?"

That's what he called his penis, "my manhood."

• • •

What's germane here is to note that the three of us got along "famously." Peas in a pod, you could say. On the surface it might appear that I had nothing in common with Bubba or Yuri. I was a Yankee blue blood by inheritance, a New England prep-school graduate, and an effete ice hockey and tennis player; I spoke three languages, and back then I was earning a modest living writing novels and a few screenplays for Hollywood. Those who didn't know better might say that I had grown up on Easy Street compared to Yuri and Bubba, a couple of working-class stiffs. Maybe. It's true that my Puritan ancestors came over on the Mayflower, and my great-grandfather times five signed the Declaration of Independence for New York State. Yet I come from a dysfunctional side of the family that was always broke, and my mother had perished in a car accident (with my dad, drunk, behind the wheel) when I was three. Subsequently, my father endured multiple harrowing remarriages and a checkered career in the CIA before he keeled over at fifty-four of a major heart infarction. Re my own qualifications, I had rheumatic fever as a child, a heart murmur as a result, and I suffered from life-threatening asthma, which never slowed me down. I should add that nobody but *nobody* gets to publish novels *and* earn a salary from Hollywood without paying dues and working their fingers down to the bone. Though I probably have piddling talent, I am a *fanatical* worker.

I may not look it on the surface—for example I'm tall, I'm lanky, I wear glasses, and my chest is concave—but you have to be careful with me because despite the so-called silver spoon I was born with in my mouth, I'm tough.

• • •

9

This is also curious—Yuri, Bubba, and I had literature in common. Put simplistically, my teen heroes had been Hemingway, Scott Fitzgerald, Carson McCullers, Thomas Wolfe—the usual suspects for a person of my generation and "privileged" background. Yuri's idols were Dostoevsky, Tolstoy, Isaak Babel, and James T. Farrell. Bubba worshipped Dan Jenkins, Tank McNamara, and Alex Karras. Actually, I'm being too hard on Bubba. I'm being snide because he seemed like such an easy target (which he was not). Truth is, he also admired short story writers like Raymond Carver, Donald Barthelme, and Flannery O'Connor. At Texas Tech Bubba had studied Shakespeare and Joseph Conrad. He was the only starter on the football roster who had read *The Caucasian Chalk Circle*. Correction: he was the only person in *Texas* who had opened a volume of Bertolt Brecht. Converse with him long enough and he might surprise you every minute. Contrary to first impressions, Bubba was nowhere near as easy to cram in a Styrofoam box as a carryout cheese burrito from Taco Bell. He was not a caricature.

Although all three of us wanted to be novelists, at the start of the Annual Big Arsenic Fishing Contest in 1983 only I had realized that dream. My first book (published in 1965) had been a campus best seller; the movie version starred Miriam Lang. My third novel was a comical diatribe against racial inequality. My fifth published work was a grim effort castigating the Vietnam War. Yes, as I "matured" I developed a Social Conscience, although that oddball attribute never had much application to our fishing contest. I'm telling you now that I am an anti-imperialist eco-Nazi who used to call myself a Marxist-Leninist. A *Groucho* Marxist-Leninist I often decreed, just for the laughs. Without a sense of humor you can't undermine the capitalist system. "Always throw the first pun" if you want to break the ice with a crowd. That's *my* motto.

One of the novels Yuri had been rewriting for many years recalled the inner-city Philadelphia of his tormented youth. "Sort of a knock-off of Henry Roth," he explained. "*Call It Sleep*, featuring Studs Lonigan and the Amboy Dukes." Yuri respected Nelson Algren; he demanded that I read *The Man with the Golden Arm*. He also forced me to complete *Pedagogy of the Oppressed*, the collected oeuvre of Frantz Fanon, *Jean-Christophe*, and Ida Tarbell's muck-raking exposé of Standard Oil and John D. Rockefeller. On the other hand, the times I critiqued Yuri's own books were painful for both of us because I felt I must tell the truth as I saw it, which was never very upbeat. To this observer, my pal's fatal flaw was that he created perfect sentences drained of spontaneity by his endlessly tortured rewriting. He worked so hard to be *great* that he squandered the viable mediocrity that might have worked. I'd like to produce superb literature myself; however, my lethal defect is that I yearn to "entertain" as well. It's like Tourette's syndrome with me.

"I don't care how much you don't like what I'm tryin' to do," Yuri would reply. "One of these days I am going to publish a book that nobody will ever forget." Then he pinched my cheeks hard and kissed me on the mouth in gratitude for attempting to set him straight.

And Bubba had voluble plans to write a Texas football

11

epic told like *The Catcher in the Rye* that climaxed in a tragic love affair, which I'll explain in a minute.

• • •

First off, though, how we all met is interesting. Initially, Yuri and I had crossed paths circa 1964 when I was being a gifted tyro in New York City's Greenwich Village, and Yuri had a fascinating girlfriend he'd met at a Johns Hopkins graduate program (in creative writing) who was living in my tenement a block south of Houston Street. Yuri would visit her on the weekends, driving up from Philadelphia on his large BMW motorcycle, his buff little torso engulfed within a World War II bomber jacket like a mini Marlon Brando.

The girl's name was Priscilla. Priscilla Endicott. She was a cagey gofer at a Wall Street brokerage firm. When Yuri got her pregnant, because I had money (having just sold my first novel) I offered to pay for the abortion she wanted. A gift, not a loan. In those days, before *Roe v. Wade*, abortions were illegal and a life-threatening nightmare unless you had enough money to afford a decent procedure with a bona fide doctor who knew what he or she was doing. Hence, Priscilla was very grateful for my largesse. Afterward, though, she cut loose from Yuri and evaporated and neither of us ever saw her again. That's how I met Yuri. We liked each other. Mutt and Jeff.

After that, whenever Yuri came to New York we'd kick back in the San Remo or at the Kettle of Fish or on a Washington Square park bench and shoot the breeze about literature, striped bass, left-wing politics, and sports. "At last the Jews have an antidote to Hitler," Yuri said. "And his name is Sandy Koufax."

He and I could wallow in sports trivia. Johnny Podres winning game seven for the Dodgers against the Yankees in 1955, Mantle and Maris chasing Babe Ruth's home run record the summer of 1961, Robin Roberts and Philadelphia's "Whiz Kids" of 1950. We also attended movies at the Bleecker Street Cinema where Yuri introduced me to Pier Paolo Pasolini, Pontecorvo's *The Battle of Algiers* and *Burn*, Antonioni's *La Notte* and *L'Avventura*. I didn't know beans about foreign films until Yuri opened that door. Thanks to him I developed crushes on Jeanne Moreau, Claudia Cardinale, Monica Vitti, and Giulietta Masina (in *La Strada*). I did not know all that much about art and politics, either. When we attended a showing of *On the Waterfront* and Elia Kazan's name appeared in the opening credits, Yuri spit at the screen. Thus I learned about HUAC, naming names, and the Hollywood blacklist. Later, "Listen to this anti-union crap!" Yuri hissed. "The whole stupid movie's his apologia for being a stool pigeon."

Yuri had more culture dancing around his thumbnail than I had absorbed in a lifetime. "I've read *Anna Karenina* twice," he said, holding up two fingers practically shoved into my nostrils. "Let me repeat that: *twice*." Yuri was Vittorio Gassman to my Jean-Louis Trintignant in *The Easy Life*. He was my Zorba the Greek. When we met I had been laid just once. Whereas by the time he graduated high school Yuri had experienced carnal knowledge with almost a dozen partners. "What is the 'secret'—?" he replied to my embarrassed query. "Just start talking to them about *anything*—Hans Castorp, washing machines, rose petals."

The fact is, Yuri forced me to educate myself, open my eyes; he changed my life by introducing me to the *real* world history and culture that has shaped our planet over the last few hundred years. I balked at first because back then you didn't graduate from an elite New England prep school and a Little Ivy college wearing a hammer and sickle baseball cap and with a snootful of dialectical materialism coming out of your nostrils every time you sneezed. I'm not saying Yuri didn't have a sense of humor, because he could tell you a fistful of jokes about a priest, a rabbi, and a Las Vegas hooker walking into a gay bar run by a stuttering dwarf, but his serious persona could hand you back your ignorance on a platter of scorn so caustic that you'd immediately want to straighten up and fly right. And I came to love him for that even though sometimes I just wished he would shut up. Yuri had something to say about *everything.* He could hold forth on Cuban cigars, Russian samovars, Pythagoras, the Spanish Inquisition, Florida grapefruits, Schopenhauer, alligator gars, Philadelphia's own Willie Mosconi, the life expectancy of Texas armadillos, American racism, modern art, the US satrapies of Central America, Antonio Gaudí's Sagrada Familia, and the 1962 welterweight bout in which Emile Griffith killed the Cuban boxer Benny "Kid" Paret, perhaps for calling him a *maricón* at the weigh-in.

Later, after I moved out west, Yuri visited me every autumn for several weeks, during which we'd fish the Río Grande, go grouse hunting up Pot Creek, or camp at alpine lakes catching fat cutthroat trout and drinking blackberry brandy in our tent at night while reading aloud to each other passages from Ernest Hemingway or from Norman Maclean's novella, *A River Runs Through It.* The ghetto brat and the preppy aesthete. By 1983, when the Annual Big Arsenic Fishing Contest began, we had a serious male-bonding history. Yuri was my best friend.

• • •

Bubba and I did not cross paths until four years after I had reached northern New Mexico in 1970. He banged on my door one day shortly after my first divorce (from Gretchen) eager to talk literature. I was thirty-four by then, still suffering from asthma and a worsening heart murmur, and Bubba was eleven years my junior, a brash twenty-three-year-old rogue fresh out of college, torn between becoming a famous novelist or robbing his first million. He had arrived in my town from Texas chasing a glamorous filly, a Dallas woman nine years his elder on the lam from her nasty ex-husband and eager to ski New Mexico. She had money, and she had been a psychotherapist to the Red Raider football team. Too, she was superficially brilliant and went by the name of Jill Terrell. Though I don't know exactly how she and Bubba had gotten involved, I do know how it ended. Jill dropped him like a lead ingot when she flew to Cancún with an Austrian chef from up in the ski valley who was also world-class in the giant slalom.

After Jill escaped from the ministrations of his rapacious manhood, Bubba had a broken heart for about forty-eight hours, then he decided to cash in by writing a roman à clef about his football experience at Texas Tech that had ended with the tragic broken heart. I forget how he learned where I lived. The pertinent fact is that I already had a modest reputation recently enhanced by the publication of my third novel, and Bubba was drawn to anybody who might help him gain an advantage in life, no matter how much of a longshot. They say some people will fuck a woodpile if they think a snake is hiding in it. I guess I was the woodpile.

Bubba was so bald-faced and funny I cottoned to him immediately. He was truly larger than life. I had never been friends with a guy from his culture and milieu. Plus, I'm a writer and it struck me immediately that Bubba could be an unforgettable brazen character in one of my future works. Turnabout woodpiles is fair play. Truth be told, I am not only a fanatical worker but also a vehement opportunist. In my trade that's a given. Yes, there are devil horns protruding from my cranium that I like to pretend are only harmless nubs. You can judge for yourselves as we proceed. I will admit up front that people like me do *not* get seventy-two virgins in Heaven.

Bubba and I hit it off and for starters he ordered me to go dove hunting with him up on the Colorado border with New Mexico where large fields of hops, barley, and other grains are harvested each autumn by combines chugging across the flat lands into the midnight hours. Most of those combines are working for the Coors Brewing Company. Somehow Bubba had become chums with one of their executives who invited him to scorch the land with three-inch Winchester #8 express loads. Chasing after doves with Bubba often left me half-autistic from trepidation because he handled a cocked shotgun as if it were a band majorette's twirling baton. Hence I bowed out of those excursions early on. I may be a lunatic but I'm not crazy.

The lad was a good shot who did not often pause to behold the flair of our natural surroundings when doves were flying by begging to be annihilated. You might compare Bubba to Arnold Schwarzenegger—the Predator, the Terminator, the *Ex*terminator, a cyborg killing machine. And if occasionally a Canadian goose or other migrating waterfowl mistakenly flew too low overhead, Bubba blasted it out of season. I never understood why, but paying $29.00 for a hunting license plus a wildlife stamp was beyond his comprehension, even though he'd willingly spring for a hundred-dollar dinner at Oglevie's afterward.

Bubba and I played tennis, too. When he asked me to teach him the game, I demurred. "Bubba, you're the worst tennis player I've ever met." He had never wielded a racket before. However, "I'm a natural athlete," he insisted. "I will bust your chops in six weeks."

Not quite. For the first year I slaughtered him six-zip, six-zip whenever we laced up our Nikes. Mercifully, I hit the ball to him with every stroke and after a few months he managed occasionally to swat it back toward me. In due course we experienced rallies that I extended as long as possible before cramming the ball down his throat. I rarely allowed him to gain points because I understood that if you gave Bubba an inch he would eventually take a country mile. Meanwhile, I enjoyed blowing him off the court. He *deserved* to be obliterated.

Don't ask me why Bubba admired the game and was so determined. Inbred athletic masochism, I suppose. For a spell we bumped heads two or three times a week, even clashing during rainstorms or falling snow, which, I admit, was fun. Tennis and blizzards go together like crepes suzette and monster truck rallies, but we basked in that dichotomy.

"I'm gaining on you," Bubba snorted when he actually stole a game off me about fourteen months into our high-altitude regime. "Your days are numbered, buddy. Guns up!"

"Guns up!" was the rally cry of the Texas Tech football team. Whenever he said it, Bubba made a gun of his right hand, index finger pointed straight and his thumb cocked like the hammer on a revolver. Basically, that gesture means, *Up yours, we're gonna win.*

I can't deny that Bubba had begun to amass a few skills between the service lines. The boy had tenacity. I no longer tendered him any charity points or returned shots directly onto his racket, preferring instead to run him ragged right to left and right again, then crush my overhead slams to the opposite sides of his court. Bubba, wrong-footed, tripped all over himself like a very comical, very spastic clown. And my serve now spun toward him twenty miles an hour faster, then I rushed the net more often to make him look stupid with cruelly executed volleys.

No mercy, no quarter. Not with this guy.

Despite my best efforts, Bubba eventually began to hold his own. He figured out how to serve, slice, chop, and effect a topspin. This forced me to wake up, winning our matches 6–3, 6–2, and then having to sweat a tad in order to triumph 6–4, 6–3. The shrewd little weasel had begun catching up to me when I wasn't paying strict attention. He was not an apathetic simpleton who just muddled along happy to carry home consolation prizes. You could never take Bubba for granted. He had an instinct for your weaknesses, especially if they were magnified (and simultaneously downplayed) by your superiority complex.

I liked and admired that in him. We were kindred. And he soon became my other best friend.

• • •

Before he could take a set off me or write his football tale, Bubba distracted himself by opening, in my town, his first Racket Ranch, which was actually a sleazy bunch of hot tubs in private rooms that horny couples could rent by the half hour to have sex in. As we became closer friends, I did serve briefly as his literary mentor of sorts, a highly unsuccessful enterprise. Bubba listened to me about as much as a grizzly bear sow with two cubs might listen to the command "Halt!" if you had crossed her path munching on a pastrami sandwich.

Pretty quickly my town grew way too small for Bubba, being that he was an exceptionally diligent entrepreneur. He expanded up to Denver and then down to Dallas and Austin, then over to Phoenix and so forth, a very busy lad. Yet we stayed in touch. Bubba liked to drop by once or twice per annum, crack a bottle of Jack, chase trout on the Río Grande, maybe slay a few birds, and then engage in tennis marathons that were not so easy for me to brush off anymore. Without informing me, the evil schemer had taken lessons from some country club pros up north. Never trust an erstwhile noseguard.

He rarely stayed for long, though, before flitting off to more important distractions. Still, over the years on my turf Bubba accumulated the hot tub bordello, a slew of rental condos, and a partial share in our new nine-hole golf course and rinky-dink private country club—small pickings. Nobody gets rich where I live, not even the rich people.

One year, when my Philadelphia pal Yuri was out west on safari with yours truly, Bubba showed up and tagged along for kicks. We were scouting elk after grouse season high on the Río Chiquito, creeping along game trails at ten thousand feet among the golden aspen groves and spruce trees. No, I have never shot an elk; yes, I have many friends who like to know where they are at when the state lottery is over. And by then I knew three watersheds in a thirty-square-mile region better than I knew my own living room, and I enjoyed leading my friends to certain elk wallows and to old bear dens and to places where I knew of a goshawk nest. I was born to be Natty Bumppo.

About five minutes after they met Yuri called Bubba "an inbred illiterate hillbilly with an IQ of two." Blatant rowdies grated on Yuri big-time (yours truly excepted), and Bubba was a blatant rowdy. That said, however, Bubba made Yuri stop, straighten up, and take a closer look because so much Texas balderdash emanating from Bubba's stocky body had a mesmerizing effect. To me, later, Yuri compared Bubba to an old-fashioned steam engine chugging across the American prairie at full throttle plowing through vast buffalo herds, knocking the bison aside off its cowcatcher like so many tenpins in a bowling alley. We agreed that Bubba was an infant incarnation of the insatiable economic life force that is transforming our planet, and, as such, he was an irresistible study and a fascinating human being.

Bubba told me that on first inspection he'd taken Yuri for a phony-baloney loudmouth poseur from the planet Mars. I informed Bubba that when he glowered at Yuri he was looking in the mirror at an exact reflection of himself except that Yuri was intelligent and also possessed a soul.

Bubba said, "And you say he's a commie rat bastard?"

"He is a socialist. He never carried a card. His parents were in the party."

Bubba challenged Yuri to a game of straight cowboy pool. I knew for a fact that Bubba possessed talent in that realm because he had crushed me shooting eight ball more times than I care to remember as easily as the proverbial knife goes through butter. I'm flat out no good at pool, and never will be, so his superiority was not an issue. Nevertheless, "I don't think you should pick a fight against Yuri," I advised Bubba. "He will eat you alive."

Bubba fell for the bait. It's so easy to sucker an egomaniac.

Back then, the only regulation pool table in our town occupied a small playroom just off the Chile Sagrado Bar at the Holiday Inn. Carefully, Yuri tested all the cue sticks in the rack before selecting one, then he spent aeons chalking the tip until Bubba grew impatient. "Come on, come on. I haven't got all night."

Yuri raised his left eyebrow. "I'll spot you twenty-five balls, Bubba, and you can have first break."

Bubba was no fool; he accepted the balls and the break and promptly lost the contest to Yuri so fast it made his ears whistle, 50–26. The Texas cowboy couldn't believe it. Yuri was a freakin' *professional* hustler.

"I'm gonna tell you something," Yuri said quietly, recounting the money Bubba had handed over after Yuri kindly reminded him that he was ten bucks short and snapped his fingers twice, impatiently, for the rest of the vig. "God forbid you should actually listen to me, since people from your neck of the planet are actually born deaf. However, even you should realize that if somebody in a pool hall who's not high on grain alcohol or Jack Daniels spots you twenty-five balls and the initial break, you need to apologize for challenging them in the first place, save your money, and offer to buy them a drink and a plate of calamar tapas instead. In my book you're like one those naïve teenage sycophants who offers to whack the senile Mafia don from the other family before they've even learned to fire a slingshot, let alone a .32 police special at close range like it's done back east. Frankly, you're so stupid my mother could beat you on a billiard table and she's never even played the game. Capeesh?"

That speech sure fired up Bubba's admiration and it cemented his friendship with my pal from Philadelphia.

For his part (as he slipped the fifty dollars carefully into his wallet), Yuri couldn't believe that Bubba had swallowed his phony gangster hogwash hook, line, and sinker, but he decided to let it ride. There's a schlemiel born every minute.

And so the three of us became a trio—Wynken, Blynken, and the prep-school *tiburón*.

· · ·

Not too long after that we decided to initiate our fishing contest on the Río Grande up at a place called Big Arsenic Springs, a beautiful location one hour north of my front door occupying a section of the watercourse declared by Congress in 1968 to be the nation's first "Wild River." The gorge was deep and fairly wide at that point, the cliff walls impressive. You could stand on the rim at the Big Arsenic trailhead gazing down at the trickle of river far below and be totally awed by the grandeur, the panorama, the all-out melodrama. It was like a pint-sized Grand Canyon and it took your breath away.

Beginning at the trailhead, piñon and juniper trees flanked a path that descended down the precipitous canyon walls to the Big Arsenic Springs. There were dozens of switchbacks. Tall ponderosa pines lined the steep track as well. We always stopped to sniff the bark of the biggest ponderosa, which usually smelled strongly of vanilla, so we dubbed it the Vanilla Tree. Great rock slides tumbled below the cliffs to the shoreline of the river itself, which was littered on both sides by basalt boulders that we crawled over like tiny crabs on immense petrified testicles. Slender willows and wild milkweed grew along the shoreline, also poison ivy, Apache plume, and rabbitbrush. The lush riparian habitat on both sides of the river supported deer and bobcats and raccoons, beaver and muskrats. Many species of ducks either nested there or passed on by, along with Canada geese and a few grebes. The area was *rich*.

We started the fishing contest as a lark, a one-year deal. Quickly, however, it grew on us to mythic proportions. Let me interject right here, right at the start, that no true sportsman ever "competes" in the killing game. I consider myself an ethical fisherman and a conscientious hunter as well. Yet I'm not sure I could make a case for myself on the one day a year that Bubba, Yuri, and yours truly plied our skills on the Río Grande eager to ace our competition. It's not that we plundered countless innocent wild souls from those waters during our annual forays. However, our out-of-context behavior is not something I'd recommend to anyone concerned about the future of this planet. That might be the point I'm attempting to make over the following pages. I hope you can bear with me. Just don't try these tricks at home.

Midway through one of his deep-sea angling adventures chasing sailfish in the Pacific for *Salt Water Sportsman*, Yuri had purchased a large wooden fish carved and brightly painted in Puerto Vallarta, Mexico. He donated it for our trophy. That fish would be like the Stanley Cup. Whoever won it was entitled to keep it for a year. We also decided that a banquet would highlight the finish of every battle. Losers to spring for the champagne, of course, and it had to be stellar grappa, preferably Möet et Chandon. There must be lewd females at the debauchery, also, and they would be required to wear immoderately slinky dresses, garter belts and stockings, spiked high heels. Fake eyelashes were optional.

Wait, don't start. Of course the women did not have to dress that way, I'm only kidding. I'm a feminist, a pro-choice advocate, and a former house husband. But when you live in a PC age like ours where 70 percent of America believes the world is flat and was designed by God in six days five thousand years ago, and the other 30 percent is locked into what the novelist Philip Roth has called an "ecstasy of sanctimony," don't you think it might be fun, once per annum, to outrage and befuddle the Yahoos with a Hooters wet T-shirt contest judged by a trio of male chauvinist piglets covered in trout slime? Push come to shove, all of us, including the bright-eyed wenches who shared our revelry, were just on the prod for some irreverent fun. Who on earth could righteously deny us that?

Two

Our first official Big Arsenic contest took place on September 22, 1983. Remember that date. We always competed in the early autumn when the Río Grande would most likely be running low and clear before the heavy freezes of late October to mid-November put the kibosh on the trout. That September 22 was a crisp day with blue skies and lovely white clouds, the kind of day you could take home to Mom with a confident smile, maybe even marry. Veins of yellow aspen trees streaked the high slopes of the Sangre de Cristo Mountains, which already had a powder of snow decorating their jagged peaks. Entire flotillas of sandhill cranes were heading south for the Bosque del Apache below Socorro, a wildlife refuge in New Mexico near the Trinity Site where Oppenheimer and company exploded the first atomic bomb. Among the sandhills in those days traveled a dozen whoopers who are no more (which is a pity I won't go into here). On the mesa west of town, migrating doves were landing at stock tanks, competing for the scant water with ibises, avocets, and quirky phalaropes. All nature was in motion along the

Río Grande Flyway that cuts down through the heart of my county.

We drove north from town in my 1980 Dodge D150 extended-bed pickup truck (with two gas tanks), drinking beer and eating swiss cheese and baloney sandwiches, and insulting each other in an obscene gangsta vernacular that is called "playing the dozens." As far as I know, the dozens evolved from black corner-boy ghetto epithets and trash talking, an abrasive but effective way of showing affection for, or competition with, other slum dwellers who understand the game. Let me emphasize "affection." Yuri had grown up with that razzing style, and Bubba also. I arrived at the dozens circuitously later in life, although once I understood the drill I adapted to it like fire ants and kudzu have adapted to the South. Raised in an uptight Puritan family (and culture), I spent my first twenty years champing at the bit eager to transform myself with vulgarity. So when the opportunity arose you had better believe I snatched it.

Yuri was my mentor, my guide, my Svengali when it came to pitching slurs. He couldn't order a Novy lox and cream cheese onion bialy in a Jewish deli on Sunday morning's Orchard Street in Manhattan without complaining that the Hasids were shortchanging him on the skimpy meat portion, and he wanted a fresh bialy—not that stale penicillin-covered, non-kosher bun—and he should call the Waffen SS because of the outrageous price the pikers were charging, out-kiking a kike. It astonished me when everybody laughed and concluded these transactions by shaking hands, maybe even pinching each other's cheeks. "Mazel tov, bubele."

Bubba couldn't *not* try to psych us out with the insult game, even if nothing was on the line. Jockeying for position was as inherent to him as wearing his white Stetson cowboy hat or pressing a finger against one nostril to blow snot from his nose onto your shoes when he had a cold. So as I drove us north that day he attacked Yuri and me with adolescent gusto, dumping on our lack of virility, our failure to produce decent incomes, our ethnic backgrounds, our Yankee stupidity. He accused me of driving too slowly, "like a nervous little old lady." He censured Yuri for having an "ego bigger than the Empire State Building." His puerile maunderings weren't even clever enough to deserve a retort, so we rolled our eyes and stared out the windshield ignoring him, the height of disdain. When Bubba kept it up, Yuri joked caustically, "Your insults are like a gentle caress."

Then, off on a tangent, Bubba prattled at length about all the girls he had recently scored with even though he'd been married for the last three years to a sensational dame named Tawanda, who was the vice-president of a Denver aromatherapy chain. Their beguiling toddler, Felicity Marie, was more spoiled than Lisa Marie Presley had been at the height of her bizarre childhood. "She's cuter than a cricket, by God," Bubba bragged.

However, in all the subsequent years that I fished and partied with Bubba, I never met his wife or the adorable daughter. Tawanda always remained out of sight in Colorado, babysitting the kid and redecorating their McMansion with Louis Quatorze furniture and faux Byzantine drapes and overseeing Felicity Marie's accordion and harpsichord lessons after she grew a bit older, although that was before the anorexia hit. The only explanation Bubba ever gave about his wife's absence from our fishing shenanigans was this:

"Listen, I love Tawanda. She is a remarkable human being and a beautiful mother to our child. In her own racket she clears over a hundred grand a year after taxes, she's got brains, she's funny, she can be a real stubborn negotiator in a business deal. She's also without question the sexiest woman I've ever known. When I'm on the road I yearn to be back with her. When she's on the road I can't wait until she returns. That said, it's a fact of life: you have to be in love and married to raise a kid, but nobody can live without strange."

• • •

Four miles above the molybdenum mining town of Questa I turned west, driving through the half-deserted settlement of Cerro onto BLM property where the paved road curled southward running parallel to the gorge rim for ten minutes in the picturesque sagebrush and piñon Wild River area that gave us all the shivers. Sunflowers and purple asters lined the route, with Guadalupe Mountain to the left and Chiflo Mountain to the right on the other side of the canyon. At the Big Arsenic trailhead atop the gorge we hopped out of my truck and posed for the first official Big Arsenic portrait. I had brought along my Nikon FE and a tripod because I sensed we were destined to be immortal and wanted a record for my offspring after I expired. I am sentimental like that. Hence, I made several timed exposures of we three heathens lined side by side holding our rod cases pointing up from our crotches toward the camera like enormous hard-ons. Lock up the women and children!

We were big fellows ready to rape the river. I contemplate those pictures today: they make me laugh they are so vivacious and innocent. We sure were full of ourselves, weren't we? And that's how it would be on the day of the Annual Big Arsenic Fishing Contest, which became our Super Bowl and much more fun. All three of us were determined, repeatedly, to be Joe Namath.

After the official portrait, we took off down the steep dirt path that wound for about a mile until it reached the river. Spiny lizards darted out of our way and yerba de chivato bloomed yellow in bushy bouquets. It seemed there were always lazy buzzards circling high overhead, my good luck charms. En route we kissed the Vanilla Tree and Yuri said, "Smell that elixir, boys." During future Big Arsenic contests that phrase became his mantra. Bubba and I made a great show of inhaling the rich vanilla odor of that tree, although I faked it a bit because the bark triggered my asthma, which in turn kicked my heart arrhythmia into gear.

A quarter mile above the Big Arsenic Springs our trail forked, sending a lateral path south for a half mile across a narrow sagebrush plateau covered by prickly pear cactus, a scattering of cholla, and many yucca plants. Then it dropped to the Little Arsenic Springs located a mile downriver from our eventual destination at Big Arsenic. At the fork we removed our rods from their aluminum cases and stashed the cases beneath a large juniper tree. We would retrieve the rod cases at night on our way back up from the Big Arsenic Springs. In other words, we would hike (and fish) in a circle.

The official contest stretch of river ran from Little Arsenic Springs north to Big Arsenic. It was a section defined by dark boulders, some boulders higher than a man, gardens of boulders. Shallow channels and gushing waters slalomed around the boulders, smashing against them, tumbling over them, always boulders. The boulders framed and populated a variety of pools, back eddies, shallow riffles, and frothy waterfalls. All of that stretch was noisy and misted by spindrift with but a few narrow beaches, and only three wider spaces of incongruously quiet water.

High canyon walls rose steeply from the opposite shore, the west side of the river. Along the eastern bank that we would travel upstream, juniper trees survived among millions of rocks often camouflaged by bright red Virginia creeper vines and tangles of gone-to-seed cottony tufted clematis. Bleached chunks of driftwood, some the remains of entire uprooted trees, lay scattered in the rubble. Occasional ponderosas stood like majestic sentinels. Above them towered the eastern cliffs that were every bit as impressive as the western canyon walls.

"Just another day in Paradise," I always said.

"My sentiments exactly," Yuri always replied.

"Bring it on!" Bubba exclaimed. "I *dominate* this puny creek!"

• • •

As soon as we reached the river on September 22, 1983, it started. Or rather, Bubba activated his spiel. And the spiel never changed, not once during the entire melodramatic run of the Annual Big Arsenic Fishing Contest. When we gathered at the shore to rig up, Bubba ordered me to tie him three leaders because his fingertips were too stubby for the task. I encouraged him to go screw himself, but was forced to relent when he threatened to boycott the contest if I didn't help him. He was jerk enough to make good on the threat. Bubba had never obtained what he desired by kowtowing to geeks. So I constructed the leaders for him composed of 6X and 8X strands of monofilament, using a complicated blood knot to join the dropper length residing a few feet up-line from the tail fly. A dropper is a fly that attracts the trout, then they'll gobble the tail fly below it. Just as often they take the dropper fly instead, but it's a trout thing so don't try to figure it out.

Next, even before we "wet our flies," something was wrong with Bubba's new reel purchased at Los Ríos Anglers that morning because he'd forgotten most of his equipment in Colorado. Bubba *always* left most of his paraphernalia at home. Why? "I travel a lot, I'm a distracted man." Or, "My valet forgot to pack my gear in the car. He has less brains than a newt on a dissecting table in a high school biology lab." Naturally, Bubba wanted me to convert his new reel from right-handed cranking to left-handed action, and I did that, taking the spool off its spindle and rotating the pawls, which reversed the winding direction of his line. Bubba had no clue how to perform this simple task himself because he had zero patience for the little details. His excuse? "I am master of the macroscopic overview."

Then Bubba demanded I supply him with the proper artificial flies for the day's event. When I suggested he could jump in the river because "you should have bought your own flies," Bubba screamed that I would forfeit the contest due to unsportsmanlike conduct. And when I say "screamed," I do mean "screamed." Constraint was not his copilot. Bubba was like an adamant baby bird squawking to be fed his worms, and he did not care if he jostled his siblings clear of the nest. In fact, that was the point. And when I refused to hand over the flies, Yuri interjected, "Bubba's right, give him the flies. And give me some also. Then let's get started."

Yuri was practical.

Outnumbered, I yielded, parceling into their sweaty palms the woolly boogers, black badgers, gold-ribbed hare's ears, peacock nymphs, partridge hackle Adams, maybe a spruce matuka. Why not be altruistic with my buds when I knew I could drub them? Plus, I'll be honest—the fish we stalked were not sophisticated; they were not permit tailing on the sand flats off of Key West or Eleuthera in the Bahamas, hence most any creation could work. I had a rule of thumb: "Little black fly, little brown fly on the dropper." If that stratagem did not produce, start experimenting. Trout brains are the size of corn kernels; human brains are almost as large as the brains of sperm whales and elephants. Ergo, who would *you* bet on?

• • •

Eventually, we were ready to commence our initial skirmish, lined along the river, each one of us placed at an individual pool fifty yards north of the Little Arsenic Springs. Yuri carried a classic wicker creel for his fish, I toted a damp burlap gunnysack tied around the left shoulder strap of my knapsack, and Bubba stored trout ignominiously in the rear compartment of his fishing vest. This habit destroyed the fish pressed against his perspiring backbone, although Bubba did not give a hoot—he was oblivious, he never ate them anyway. Trout for him were bragging rights, nothing more, like the size of his Texas-sized manhood.

Yuri said, "Bubba, that's no way to carry a fish. You'll make it inedible."

Bubba's snarky rejoinder was, "So what—do fish have souls?"

Yuri raised one hand in rebuke. "Hold on a sec. After college I worked as a waiter in high-class restaurants for years in order to earn a living. I'm not talking about the corner luncheonette or a cracker Toddle House in your neck of the woods. I carried a card for the Restaurant Workers Union. I wore a tuxedo and a spotless white apron while I prepared steak flambé at the table. I said 'at the table.' People paid for good food and they got their money's worth. The restaurants took care of the red meat, the chicken, the halibut, and the shellfish. Because victuals were tasty and the service excellent, I could make a decent wage off tips. I don't care how ignorant you are, you ought to learn respect for the viands we consume."

Bubba replied with a cryptic obscenity referring to the act of fellatio.

We went to work at the moment midafternoon shadows mottled the river's surface. You fish wet flies, high, on the Río Grande, you need those shadows on the water to bring up the prey. In bright sunshine trout remain deep and you have to nymph for them, which was not our style. I skittered my flies across wider pools, zigzagging the dropper on the surface like an emerging caddis fly; I cast upstream and retrieved a dead drift; I cast downstream and jerked my rig up against the currents imitating a wounded minnow. At certain key spots I flung my tufts of feather and hair thirty feet to the opposite shore where eager quarry lay up against the overhangs. I hopped onto many boulders out among the currents in order to essay presentations from various angles so that I pretty much covered the many ways sustenance traveled on those currents to hungry predators. And immediately I began catching fish.

"You cheater!" Bubba yelled when he saw my rod bending with a telltale quiver. "That was my fish. You lose a point. *You robbed my pool, you thief!*"

His outrage was kneejerk, automatic, not even emotional. It was a game, mindless aggression he hoped might rattle me, placing me on the defensive. I quickly surmised that Bubba's protests would be a Greek chorus dogging me throughout that afternoon (and throughout the many years of our fishing contest). My reaction—?

"Two points for me," I called to Bubba over the river's roar, clonking the twelve-inch brown trout against a rock and slipping it into my gunnysack. The extra point was for landing the first fish of the afternoon. Then I dipped the sack into the river before twisting the neck and tying it again to a portion of the knapsack shoulder strap under my left armpit. The wet fish banged against my hip and it felt good. Why? Because there's nothing sweeter than meat in the freezer.

That's what makes America great.

We three alternated pools, shambling upriver fairly close together, fishing our hearts out. I caught trout often, horsing them through the foam, netting them quickly and banging them senseless if they were respectable keepers. No mercy from this Philistine. Fishing contests aren't about the aesthetics of pastoral rumination, they are about "harvesting the qualifiers." In realspeak that means "killing things." And that day I hardly ever missed a strike, which was rare for me but it happens. Like Bob Beamon at the 1968 Mexico City Olympics, remember him?

By contrast, Bubba had stumbled out of bed on the wrong side of the river. He hooked a lunker and lost it. He snarled his line; he snapped off flies on his backcast; he got hung up in the willows. And he cursed the day that he was born, which was music to my ears, Gentle Reader. I was eating him for lunch.

And Yuri? He stayed preoccupied on his own quiet planet, straining to catch fish, but afraid to hop on the rocks. It behooved him to be prudent. At five three his legs were too short for serious jumping. Don't forget, he had grown up angling mostly from party boats or surfcasting the ocean from New Jersey beaches, pretty tame environments. Even today, on assignment chasing steelhead up the Klamath River or trolling for Dorado around picturesque Belize cays, he was accompanied by guides and rarely this physically challenged. Yuri could sashay fearlessly through dangerous homeboys blocking the sidewalks of an urban slum, but Río Grande boulders intimidated him. "They ain't even human," he fumed.

Still, Yuri was tough, scrupulous, punctilious. He had

honor. When his line became snarled he never asked for help, he took out his pipe and lit it and then sat patiently working to untangle the mess. He prided himself on patience and self-reliance. Often he contemplated the scenery, just happy to be there. By contrast, whenever Bubba garbled his rig he ordered me to stop fishing and come tender aid. If I refused, he hollered that it was illegal for me to fish when he could not. Bubba did not dare yell at Yuri like that because Yuri would have pulled out the Herter's bowie knife on his hip and cut Bubba a new asshole between his eyes. Me? Dripping with solicitude I always toddled over to assist His Royal Highness simply to shut him up and because I knew I could trounce him anyway, and I wanted him to know that.

• • •

We covered the rugged stretch of river from Little Arsenic Springs up to Big Arsenic where the BLM had built several cabanas and an outhouse and five new picnic tables placed on a flat bench area among a dozen juniper trees and tall ponderosas. A pretty place. Canyon wrens unleashed their diving melodies; we heard an owl hooting from high on the cliffs. Refilling our empty water bottles at the main pool, we drank greedily. The "arsenic" water wasn't poisonous, it was healthy, I forget why. Rules were we did not display the catch nor tote up points until we had arrived back home. We wanted to build up tension for the Official Unveiling at my house where our ribald companions were preparing the banquet. Not to be a killjoy, but I already knew that my fellow competitors were toast.

Up the trail we climbed, slowly, as light departed the

canyon and stars began to shine. It's an arduous, steep journey at the end of a hard afternoon. Believe me, you do not sprint up that path after a day on the river. I frequently took a squirt off my Albuterol inhaler at the start. Bubba had to keep waiting for Yuri and me, the geezers, to catch up. The Milky Way tailed north and south directly overhead; it was breathtaking. Completing a circle, we fetched our rod cases where the trail forked at the Little Arsenic spur that we had taken downstream earlier. I was grateful to have my rod case for a walking stick during the last stage of our ordeal.

On our way north in my truck along the paved Wild River access road that ran beside the edge of the canyon we drank beer and consumed potato chips. We were numbed by fatigue but felt good—it's called "the ecstasy of exhaustion." A few kangaroo rats zipped across the narrow road; two deer on the shoulder froze as we cruised by. Popping open our second beers, we began discussing Ernest Hemingway and Scott Fitzgerald like college freshman in a PX drinking coffee and munching on cinnamon crullers. Then Yuri complained about the novel he had been working on unsuccessfully for years.

I told him, "Maybe you're trying too hard."

Yuri snapped back at me, "Maybe you're not trying hard enough."

"You're too finicky," I said, not for the first time. "I've told you—type it clean, send it off, move on."

That punched his button, and when you punched Yuri's button you received an earful. I'll try to re-create the gist of his tirade because, one, it gives you an idea of the "Real Yuri," and two, because it sets the tone for my story to follow, which, you may be happy to note, is not just about catching trout on the Río Grande.

"Wait a minute you condescending popinjay," Yuri said to me. "You don't know anything about real literature. I'm not interested in blamming out a bunch of second-rate novels for little old ladies wearing Supp-hose to read in their Scarsdale gazebos after tea on Sunday afternoons. I am a *serious* person and a *serious* writer. My roots ain't Damon Runyon, Max Shulman, and that Armenian lightweight you love so much, what's-his-name, Billy Saroyan. I've read Joyce and Hugo and George Eliot and *Germinal* by Émile Zola, and Gide and Malraux and Camus. I'm sorry, but I've read *Les Misérables*, every stinking word of it, and I've read *Anna Karenina* twice and *The Brothers Karamazov* and *War and Peace*. I'm not saying that to pretend I'm some kind of elitist pansy with a phony aristocrat accent pasting up the *Paris Review* in George Plimpton's silk-stocking Manhattan apartment, either. I took those books *seriously*. Who gives a fig for Jay Gatsby with all his pretty shirts, or 'the old man and the sea' carrying his stupid sailspar like a blinking neon cross? Spare me, please. I'm interested in 'The Grand Inquisitor' and Jean Valjean and Flaubert. I said *Flaubert*. In my own work I strive to say something about the human condition that isn't mere lightweight tripe like what's-his-name, your other hero, Harold Robbins. I want to be like *Proust*. I admire Romain Rolland. I *care* about what I'm doing and the language I'm doing it in even if it takes me forever to create it, you understand? Novels that count aren't sired in a day by jackasses like you who spend all their hours pestering their agents and their editors for the royalty figures while they're negotiating film points and sitting at the Throne Table at Ma Maison. You tell me this if you can: What's the point of creating anything less than a masterpiece?"

"Harold Robbins is not my hero," I grumbled defensively.

"He's *my* hero," Bubba said. "When I write it, my football novel will be a best seller. It'll be better than anything you two Yankees ever wrote and it will go out on movie option even before it's published and I'll buy five Cadillacs with the money. They'll hire me to write the script for four hundred thousand dollars, plus two and a half percent of the shooting budget up to a million dollars. And at the back end I'll get five percent of the gross."

I stated the obvious. "Nobody gets a percent of the gross."

"Just watch me," Bubba said in a burst of what Yuri might have called "vainglorious hauteur."

I slowed down, hitting the brakes, and stopped. Right in front of us a small owl occupied the middle of the road with a tiny dead mouse at its feet. The owl had long legs and a compact body. It was about ten inches high, no ear tufts, brown with white spots. Eyes glittering from my headlights, it remained in place, hypnotized.

"What the heck is that?" Bubba asked.

"A burrowing owl," I said.

"Beep the horn."

"I don't want to scare it. Relax. It'll fly away in a second."

But the owl did not fly away. It was transfixed.

"Beep the damn horn," Bubba repeated impatiently.

"Maybe he doesn't want to beep the horn," Yuri said.

His seat was in the middle between Bubba and me. "Leave him alone. The situation will resolve itself presently."

We sat quietly staring at the blinded little fellow blocking our route.

"Maybe if you turn off the lights," Yuri suggested.

I pressed in the dash button for about ten seconds, and when I pulled out the nob the owl was gone but the mouse still lay there.

Bubba opened the passenger door, stepped down, circled in front of my truck, and cautiously picked up the mouse by its tail. Approaching the driver-side door, he lifted up the windshield wiper and pinned the mouse against the glass by lowering the wiper blade onto its tail. Then he circled around to the far door and climbed back into the truck.

"Okay," he said. "*Ándale, pendejo.*" I think those were the only two words he knew in Spanish.

"You're an infant," Yuri stated to Bubba as I accelerated. "You're going to remain neotenic for the rest of your life."

"I hope so," Bubba chortled.

Yuri grabbed Bubba in a headlock, knocking off his Stetson, and they started to wrestle while I pleaded, "Not here, not now, I'm trying to drive the truck. Cool it, you turkeys. *Grow up!*"

We three thrived on sophomoric horseplay.

· · ·

At home the girls awaited us all gussied up in over-the-top sleazy apparel with our first Annual Big Arsenic banquet arranged on platters. Yes, on the one hand they were being sarcastic sexpots; on the other hand the dinner smelled

good. A pork roast, sweet potatoes, broccoli, salad with arti-
choke hearts and tender baby stalks of asparagus. We never
devoured our fresh-caught fish at the Big Arsenic banquet
because it would have taken too long to cook them. Instead,
we wrapped the cleaned and gutted trout in aluminum foil
and popped them into the freezer for later consumption.
Right now we were hungry; we wanted to eat.

Bubba's date, Christie Mepps, was the first in a line
of interchangeable Bubba Babes that attended our post-
contest festivities over the years. She was an arrogant trophy blond from Odessa who wore an old-fashioned cocktail
dress and a rhinestone tiara in her bouffant. Turns out she
was a high-end real estate agent married to a half-blind old
codger in the oil business twice her age who kept her on
a long leash. When she tweaked her finger under Bubba's
chin, Christie called him "my little Texas buckaroo."

My bawdy consort, Louella Leyland, had on a short jersey skirt, a silken ecru blouse, and a pretty choker around
her neck. She was a cheeky travel agent who giggled a lot
from smoking doobies. We had met at a local tennis tournament that I won by a country mile (the over-forty bracket)
while she was cleaning up a younger women's draw.

And Yuri's new girlfriend, Sharon Adair, a paralegal
with a New York law firm, sported high heels, per Yuri's
instructions, black leotards, a faux fur chubby, and enough
makeup to sink the Lusitania. Standing a foot taller than
Yuri, she wore big, thick-lensed, dark-rimmed glasses and
was full of complaints.

"I feel like a whore in this froufrou outfit. I mean, when

I graduate and pass the bar I'll be one of the partners on the shingle."

"Shuttup," Yuri said, giving her butt a love pinch to make her squeal. "Quit feelin' sorry for yourself and take it like a man."

Sharon pushed his hand away, commenting, "Who are *you* going to sleep with tonight?"

The women were fun, however; they all had funky attitude and satirically hailed us as heroic returning conquerors as we popped the cork on a bottle of pricey bubbles compliments of Bubba. And when the Moment of Truth arrived, I cut down my angling pals like ripe wheat in August. Poor babies. Yuri had two ten-inch trout that barely qualified, Bubba displayed three fish with none longer than a foot, and I pulled four lunkers from my sack that measured out, on average, to sixteen inches a piece. Monsters! Christie and Louella shrieked and pranced around with exaggerated fanfare, then took turns bussing me like tarts in a Victorian farce. Though Sharon was not as overtly demonstrative, she tried to be a good sport and also planted a smack on my lips while Bubba and Yuri yelled, "Hey, hey, enough already, *cut that out!*"

Sorry, those were the rules, I was king for a day. And when our first annual bacchanalia was done, the colorful wooden fish trophy from Puerto Vallarta belonged to me for a year. I kissed it, I clasped it against my bosom, then I hung it on my kitchen wall. *Look on my fish, ye mighty, and despair.*

Purple prose alert! In the hay that night Louella slithered all over me like an erotic starfish with its hundreds of suction cups delicately nibbling my extremities top to bottom from my hammertoes to the tip of my pulsating nose, electrifying every inch of skin and muscle with her rapacious eagerness to make love with me like Julius Caesar's favorite concubine after his mighty subjugation of Gaul.

"More, more," I commanded urgently as she plied her tantalizing wiles.

"Okay, okay," she murmured huskily while I groaned in blissful agony as her moistened lips brushed across my nipples, my belly button . . . and so forth.

And as far as I was concerned, purple prose and all, the Annual Big Arsenic Fishing Contest was off to a splendid start.

Veni, vidi, vici.

Three

Of course, any reader with half a brain might say, "Wait a minute, you won that first Annual Big Arsenic contest because the cards were stacked. It was your river in your hometown in your home state. You got to fish it year round while your buddies were living thousands of miles away in Philadelphia and Denver."

And that is true, except for this consideration: The Río Grande is muddy and unfishable much of the year due to freezing winter temperatures and spring snowmelt causing high water runoff lasting well into the summer. The river is usually only low and clear for a couple of months come fall. And each autumn since 1971 when Yuri had first flown out west to hunt and fish with me, I had led him down various trails on the Río Grande and taught him all I know about how to read the water, what equipment to use, the way to cast this riffle or that back eddy. I had guided him down Caballo Trail and Suicide Slide, Rattlesnake and many other routes. They were special paths, they were difficult, and they led to fabulous areas, seldom fished. They could be white and deep, or with wide shallow riffles, or crowded with boulders, or smooth and quiet. Thanks to me, Yuri had experienced all of it, repeatedly, before we ever commenced our Big Arsenic shindig. Added up, our time spent on the river was about equal for both of us.

Too, you should not forget that Yuri had been fishing since his toddlerhood back east in salt estuaries and on Barnegat Bay, and in the Atlantic Ocean as well. And nowadays he was a professional—I repeat, Professional—angler, a sports writer who needed to know how to do it in order to describe it. He had conquered the Neversink, the Allagash, the Madison, even the Orinoco in Venezuela. Yuri had fly-fished for brook trout in Labrador, for grayling in Alaska, explaining his techniques to hundreds of thousands of readers. Maybe Yuri could seem disadvantaged on the Río Grande, but, despite his short legs and inability to leap, at heart he did not think so himself because he possessed a much wider range of experience than either Bubba or me. His experience, his wisdom, his anal-retentive concentration and memory gave him the edge.

In fact, after we had fished the Big River a few seasons together, if I endeavored to correct his technique or suggested a different approach to a riffle, Yuri quickly instructed me to, "Shuttup. I know what I'm doin'."

As for Bubba on the Río Grande?

First off, he was so arrogant about his natural-born physical and mental superiority that he assumed he could ride roughshod over any fisherman on any river in any state. Yours truly and Yuri included. Bubba had more delusions of his grandeur than Napoleon and Henry VIII together. Plus you should know that by the time our contest got under way, Bubba had angled on all the fabled trout waters out west. Repeatedly. He and his business associates and his golf cronies had profited from guided trips on the Yellowstone, the Big Blackfoot, name a famous Rocky Mountain stream. Bubba had also fished in Alaska; he'd caught trout across Canada; he once stalked lunkers on private Scottish rivulets where the deferential gillies practically fastened the sleek aquatic animals for him onto his royal olive dun.

I tried to enlighten him about the Río Grande, same as I'd hoped to instruct Yuri—but no dice. Bubba considered the Río Grande a third-rate river that he could easily conquer with his first-rate talents, ". . . so don't bug me with your grating admonitions, you provincial hick."

And maybe I should add this. Long ago I learned how to crack the Río Grande's code in just one afternoon from a local yokel who showed me the ropes. He taught me how to tie a blood knot in five minutes, and gave me a little black fly and a little brown fly for the dropper. Then he demonstrated how to "skitter" the flies, holding my rod tip high. Finally, he advised me to pass up most of the water—"Just fish to trout." I absorbed that advice over the brief time it took him to educate me. Then, off on my own during the next hour and a half, I landed seven brown trout and three rainbows even though I had flubbed nearly half my hits.

Hence I repeat: If you knew only a few basic rules, fishing the Río Grande did not even remotely qualify as rocket science. Anyone could do it. And neither Bubba nor Yuri was a neophyte. Thus the annual Big Arsenic struggle was not as lopsided as the casual reader might suspect given that it took place on my "home court," so to speak. All things considered, I figure the contest was pretty even steven, and, in case you fear that our story is just another ho-hum hook and bullet yawner, I promise you that what follows is not a run-of-the-mill angling saga tailored to the ATV, beer-drinking crowd. In fact, hang onto your hats, folks, because my plan from now on is to drive this narrative toward its astonishing and tragic denouement in much the same way that we three prepubescent misfits moved up the Río Grande, covering a lot of territory quickly, passing up most of the water, and casting only to trout.

• • •

I came very close to losing for the first time in only our third competition (on October 3, 1985) when I snapped my rod tip twenty minutes into the afternoon and nearly defaulted the match. That year Bubba was only thirty-three, Yuri and I had celebrated forty-five, I was working on two screen-plays, I'd recently published my fifth novel, and I had just married my second wife, Rachel Ivory, an intriguing and no-nonsense person with an IQ off the charts. We had met over the summer in the war-torn country of Nicaragua, which was fomenting a Sandinista revolution that was being harassed by a contra army counterinsurgency supported by Ronald Reagan's right-wing autocracy and the CIA. While on a brief film-oriented research tour there with a small group of lefties supported by a Los Angeles Jesuit coun-cil promoting Liberation Theology, I collided with Rachel, a journalist on assignment for NACLA. We initially came face-to-face crouching in a trench on the Honduran border while being debriefed by an FSLN colonel on the guerrilla contra war's situation.

I'd call it lust at first sight, no doubt heightened by the surrounding atmosphere of heroic revolution, leftist nation-building, a pending United States invasion, and the bristling array of loaded AK-47s guarding us.

Back in the USA I visited Rachel for a week at her San Francisco apartment, then she passed five intoxicating days with me in New Mexico. Three weeks after that, over a long-distance phone connection, I importuned her to marry me and she said, "Yes." I don't claim to have made a whole lot of rational decisions during my life, and that certainly wasn't one of them. I'm not being disingenuous here. "Reason" had nothing to do with our rash decision. Perhaps we tied the knot because the phone sex was great. I loved the sound of her caustic voice, and she considered my edgy sense of humor adorable. Our complementary radical politics stoked the flames.

My older daughter, Stephanie, observed, "You are so out of your comfort zone, Dad." She was sixteen. My other daughter, Naomi, asked, "Am I gonna have a stepmother who's younger than my sister?" She was twelve. Their mother, Gretchen, worked for a pottery barn operation in Albuquerque featuring popular hand-thrown porcelain vessels that reproduced John Keats's immortal Grecian urn for the gift shops of many art museums back east. About Rachel she kept mum. What good would it have availed her to kvetch about her ex-husband's prodigious immaturity?

I'm guessing that Rachel and I fantasized marriage would be like bungee-jumping off the Golden Gate Bridge locked in fevered coitus after smoking a couple of joints and dropping four tabs of purple Owsley. Obviously, we weren't thinking straight, but not thinking straight is an amazing turn on. It's so exciting to be out of control, acting impulsively on the blind spontaneity of sexual excess and the untenable lunacy embraced by swearing to cohabit together forever, which may be the most cockamamie concept humanity ever invented.

Believe me, we were both enraptured by the provocative luminosity of melodrama and its total lack of self-restraint. Just writing about it propels me into an irregular heartbeat.

Rachel was thrice divorced and the mother of two almost-grown teenage boys living in Alaska right now gill-netting salmon for competing boats. During a prior existence she had been a movie critic for the New Orleans *Times-Picayune*, the manager of a San Antonio art gallery on the River Walk, a special ed teacher on the Lower East Side of Manhattan, and a painter of diorama backgrounds at the Sam Noble Natural History Museum in Norman, Oklahoma. I know, I know. Needless to say, between marriages there had been other men. Rachel came with baggage and so did I. She was five foot six with green eyes and faintly strawberry-colored hair, a wiry body from working out (riding a bike, jogging, hiking, swimming at the gym), and a languid aura radiating off of her that captured me within an invisible physical embrace that is difficult to describe and was impossible to resist. She reeked of manic energy *and* erotic lassitude simultaneously.

I was six years older than Rachel.

That was also the year we began calling Yuri's steady

New York girlfriend, Sharon Adair, his "partner"—she had recently graduated law school and was studying to pass the bar. Yuri visited her every weekend, driving up from Philly behind the wheel of an old Chrysler Imperial. They were *serious*.

"She's got moxie," Yuri bragged.

"He's such a flattering little mensch," Sharon replied.

For our contest banquet that autumn Bubba had brought along the third of his interchangeable Bubba Babes, Cheryl Blane. Cheryl ran a big-time Denver catering service that specialized in French pastries and New Orleans étouffées. Like all of Bubba's dates, she was a good looker and athletic as well, a club champion in paddle tennis and a great golfer into the bargain. To boot, she was charismatically cheerful and a funny comedienne with attitude and a fast mouth who kept up a running patter about Bubba's wife, Tawanda.

"She hired my people to cater a luncheon at the country club for fifty women in town attending a sales convention about bagless vacuum cleaners," Cheryl said. "That's one of her lucrative sidelines. We're best friends. When I play her in paddle tennis I swear to God she would kill me to win if I ever came close to beating her. That woman is as fierce as a tornado, and she looks like a Hollywood actress. She told me once that her macho hubby had a little bald mouse the size of her pinkie, but at least there's a pile-driving ass behind it."

"Hey!" Bubba protested good-naturedly. "Hey, you're talking about my *wife*."

"And she knows you're here with *me*?" Cheryl laughed. "If she wasn't so cool in her own right maybe I'd feel sorry for her. Yet she is *not* a girl in a gilded cage, believe me." Then she reached forward and unzipped Bubba's fly, calling back over her shoulder, "Will one of you please lend me a magnifying glass?"

None of the women came fishing with us, however; you don't mix Campari with Wild Turkey 101.

Insult to injury, as we three were driving north that year, Bubba suddenly puffed up like a toad in order to announce that he had sold his *Catcher in the Rye*–type football novel the previous month for a forty-thousand-dollar advance, with another twenty Gs attached because it had already gone out on film option a year before they planned to publish it.

"You *what*?"

It was called *The Obnoxious Noseguard*, an exposé, as promised many years earlier, of Texas football. When I read it in galleys six months later I blanched because it was a good book, outrageously funny, poignant, and sad. Believe it or not, Bubba could write. And I mailed his publishers a glowing blurb, comparing the novel to *North Dallas Forty* and *The Southpaw* by Mark Harris. Bubba explained to us that he had finally penned the book over only six weeks after sending his wife, Tawanda, and the princess, Felicity Marie, off to a Scientology retreat in Palm Springs so he could have the Denver McMansion all to himself.

"Nobody writes a novel in six weeks," Yuri said. "What did you do, hire a monkey to bang on the typewriter keys all day?"

Yuri was pissed because he'd been belaboring one book for seven years and suddenly this "fat little cowboy" had knocked down forty grand for six weeks' travail? He flushed purple and the veins in his temples bulged out while he invoked the names of Tolstoy, Dostoevsky, and Camus in opposition to a literary parvenue like our brawny chum from Lubbock—Schmubbock!—who didn't know a dangling participle from a split infinitive, and who probably thought I. B. Singer was a sewing machine.

Bubba threw up his hands. "I never claimed I was Tolstoy," he asserted. "I hate Tolstoy. I put his novels instead of bricks into my toilet tanks to conserve water at every flush because I'm an environmentalist."

"You're goddam right you're not Tolstoy," Yuri said, his indignant finger waggling an inch before the front brim of Bubba's white Stetson cowboy hat. "You're not even Jackie Collins's retarded little brother. You think money makes you an artist? Well, guess again you mendacious hypocrite, *money ain't worth the paper it's printed on.*"

Bubba smirked at him. "Temper, temper, Yuri. Methinks thou dost protest too much."

Yuri swatted the white Stetson off his head. "Hey!" Bubba yelped, grabbing the precious hat in midair as his golden pretty-boy locks swished every which way.

"Get a haircut," Yuri spat. "You look like you live in a little house on the prairie."

And they began roughhousing again like boys in grammar school fighting over a candy bar, giggling to beat the band while I shouted anxiously at them to cease and desist before they caused us to crash.

Later that same day I overreacted to a big strike, yanking too hard and snapping the rod tip I mentioned earlier.

However, when I scurried upstream to inform Yuri and Bubba that we needed to postpone the contest until the next day, they balked. Bubba said, "No way, José. Tie a leader around your shriveled manhood and fish with it if you have to." And when I appealed to Yuri he said, "Quit feeling sorry for yourself and take it like a man."

Since you can't argue with Neanderthals, I spliced the broken tip to my rod using old Band-Aids sequestered in my vest, thank God. This hampered my casting so I changed my technique, going after my targets closer to shore. Fairly soon I got the hang of it and began catching fish. I.e., I started vivisecting that river like an ER surgeon in Cleveland treating gunshot wounds on Saturday night. I caught a nine-inch trout and let it go. Then I bagged an eleven incher, netting it gracefully and chucking it back into the drink. After that I hooked a large brown trout in some back-eddy foam and set it free; I eased a fine cutbow out of a riffle and released it carefully. No need to kill anything yet, I was on a roll. And I poached a few more qualifying fish, all browns, plucked from here and there, mostly on short casts to the edges of nearby rocks where my fly would be activated quickly by the speedy currents, which is exactly when the tailing brown trout struck before my imitation bugs could escape. You've heard about baseball sluggers who speak of days when they could really "see" the ball? Well, that day with my fractured rod I could really "see" the fish.

To top it all off, moments before dark I netted a nineteen-inch brown trout that probably weighed three pounds. Ten points in one fell swoop! I was home free! I had dapped a woolly worm into a crescent of foam curled around a rock at my feet, and I horsed out the startled beauty before it could gear up to run. Neither Bubba nor Yuri saw me land it, they had lagged too far downstream. I paused to admire the lunker with its jutting lower jaw and sharp teeth, its black dorsal spots and bright yolk-yellow siding and its orange ventral fins, then I conked it and slipped the trophy into my gunnysack and dampened it in the river. Lifting the dripping bag, I relished the heft of it. My sack would be heavy to carry out containing just a few behemoths. And that made me feel like a man. Naturally, I felt extra-macho because I had conquered the river (and my derisive colleagues, as it turned out) with a disabled wand.

You mess with me, I kick your butt.

Then we hied ourselves home where my buddies' licentious girlfriends and my adorable new bride fell all over me with sexy congratulatory kisses (because those were the rules), and later, after our banquet when my house was dark and Yuri, Bubba, Cheryl, and Sharon had retired to their motel, I canoodled Rachel's brains out for a couple of hours straight until finally, deliriously happy (of course!) she cried, "Uncle!"

· · ·

Four years later, however, autumn of 1989, it was me crying "Uncle!" as I fled from Rachel Ivory burned out, impotent, my tail tucked between my legs, my heart locked in atrial fibrillation, my doctors getting rich. I was forty-nine years old, maybe fatally ill, and also fearing for my career. How could marriage be so degrading and confrontational? Rachel had taken me out back to the woodshed and delivered a proper whupping. I don't want to delve into it, though just for the record I will reveal that over the previous four years I had been in an unprecedentedly volatile relationship akin to Ted Hughes and Sylvia Plath's, except I was the one ready to cram my head into the oven. Don't get me wrong, it takes two to tango and I have to admit I was a jerk. I should have been more open, more sympathetic, more *sensitive*. Sadly, my problem is I have always had a bad habit of waking up aghast when the infatuation wears off, compulsively asking myself (in terror), "Where *am* I? What *now?*"

Actually, forget that baby-talk BS. Just once I should summon enough courage to override my jealousy, my deflated ego, my broken heart. Rachel actually threw *me* out of the house because she deemed that I had total disregard for the sort of compassion needed to release the kind of vulnerability that is required to build true intimacy between a man and a woman. There were feminist hegemony issues. "You are such an uptight cad," she accused repeatedly throughout our tempestuous few years together spent constantly at loggerheads. "Why can't you understand the difference between passionate codependency and unselfish affection?" "I can't believe you shtupped one of your ex-husbands!" I shouted back at her. "It didn't *mean* anything!" she yelled. "I was just feeling bored. Love is not defined by erections. *You don't own me.*" Then for twenty minutes she spewed at me invective originally coined by Betty Friedan, Susan Brownmiller, Angela Davis, and Shulamith Firestone. "But we're *married,*" I sobbed, mortified. "We promised to be *true.*" "I *am* true," her scalding tongue insisted. "'True' has nothing to do with genitalia. You act as if tenderness is illegal. Screwing like banshees doesn't *prove* anything. Lust is fun but it's not forever. If you would honestly give yourself up to me like an adult I would respond in kind. But I can't stand your ornery obsessive desire for total control over me, you country bumpkin. *I will not be a submissive puppy in your patriarchy!*"

I beseeched her not to be that way. I knew what I was losing and couldn't bear the thought. I had become a prisoner of her typhoon. Anger is an aphrodisiac. I went down on my knees, a puling figment of my former self. The background music? "Our Maladjustment Threnody."

"Sex can only carry two people so far," Rachel said, "then they should begin using their cerebral aptitude. And not merely to protest the S and L bailout or the Exxon Valdez oil spill. Your so-called brain is still crawling through the muck of the Precambrian and it can't even breathe oxygen yet. Get out of here! Stop clinging to me. I can't stand your irrational cupidity!"

"I don't *understand* what you're *saying!*" I cried bitterly from the driveway. "You call yourself a journalist but you can't even handle words correctly!"

Tough titty. She had already slammed the door behind me.

To round out the picture, I was broke. Nay, destitute. My last two novels had been rejected and both screen projects moldering on my desk had gone into turnaround. As an aside I might mention here, solely to be candid, that Rachel's backsliding with her third ex had taken place while I was off on a dubious road trip with Bubba during the late spring of 1988. It was his habit to hit town without warning, driving something conspicuously horrendous like a disgusting black Hummer, and he would order me to stop everything, pull up stakes for a week, and indulge him on one of his joyrides "to let off steam." My radical politics aside, I had often joined him, justifying my actions, I suppose, the way the hypocritical environmental activist Ed Abbey, God bless him, had justified his male chauvinism and racism by throwing beer cans out of his truck window. (*Think* about it.)

On this particular occasion, May of 1988, Bubba and I traveled between ninety and a hundred miles an hour north to Edmonton, Alberta, for a Stanley Cup finals hockey game between the local Oilers and the Boston Bruins, our purpose being to see Wayne Gretzky—the Babe Ruth of hockey— in action, all expenses compliments of Bubba. Wayne and his phenomenal teammates obliged us by hammering the Bruins, 4–2, helped by a referee, Don Koharski, who called multiple penalties on the Beantowners. Gretzky earned assists on the first two Edmonton goals, and, with the game tied two-all in the third period, he scored the winning goal, a piece of remarkable artistry I get to remember for all time, thanks to Bubba.

Other spontaneous excursions Bubba lured me into over the years took us to the annual Diamondback Rattlesnake Jubilee roundup in Lometa, Texas, which was hands down the creepiest, craziest carnival I ever attended in my life, a true homage to the bad taste and econihilism of Texas snake handlers, snake haters, snake eaters, and snake-oil salesman.

On a subsequent blitzkrieg outing Bubba drove me at

supersonic speeds to Las Vegas where, thanks to his largesse, we bunked top floor at Caesar's Palace, attended a porn convention where Bubba paid for me to receive a French kiss from Christy Canyon, went to a show that night featuring a half-dozen transgendered Elvis impersonators, and in the morning we played tennis at his recently opened Blackjack Racket Ranch, a health spa the size of Versailles that featured water-resistant slot machines in the Grecian hot tubs and in the Roman saunas. "Rodney Dangerfield loves this place."

That was an epic tennis match. I came out on top only after fighting for my life using every trick up my sleeve. When, by sheer imperious overconfidence, Bubba finally slammed a fatal match-point overhead into the net, I capsized onto my back like Bjorn Borg or John McEnroe after winning an epic Wimbledon final. Bubba yelled, "Get up, you lucky pissant, and shake my hand like a man." His face gleamed with so much humor and confidence I could tell he understood that I was on the brink of imminent subservience to his growing skills.

Next morning we sped over to a Lathrop Wells brothel (which he had just purchased) for a five-course luncheon with the director, the madam, three accountants, a sexual health specialist, and four of the girls dressed demurely in Scottish kilts, knee-high crimson Musketeer boots, and button-up pink blouses with Peter Pan collars. I'm not sure I understood the concept, although Bubba explained he simply had to check in on management and go over the books to keep his lackeys honest.

On these road junkets we jabbered about novels, movies, sports, American culture, and sang along with Johnny

Cash, Merle Haggard, Tammy Wynette, George Jones, Bob Dylan, Neil Young, Loretta Lynn, and Dolly Parton. As a kid Bubba had lain in bed after lights-out listening quietly on his radio to Bill Mack's *Open Road* show on WBAP in Fort Worth-Dallas. "Wee Marie gave the traffic reports and Harold Taft was the 'World's Greatest Weatherman.'" The show was sponsored by Rip Griffin's truck stops. All the songs were by Jim Reeves, Waylon Jennings, Tammy Wynette, and Web Pierce. "I loved Bill Mack," Bubba said, almost forlornly.

He had total recall about everything that had occurred during his childhood. "I was the runt of the litter. When I learned to drive I had to sit on three cushions in order to see over the steering wheel. In fifth grade the kids made fun of me, they called me a 'dwarf.' At home I ran around the house twenty times after dinner to build up wind and make my legs tough. My mother, Purcine, blended me vanilla milkshakes with six raw eggs in them twice a day, for breakfast and for a snack before dinner. I mowed our lawn with a hand mower three times a week to build endurance. The grass was never more than a half-inch high. To make myself stronger I wrestled with Brian. He was a half-foot taller and twenty pounds heavier, but didn't like wrestling because I would try to kill him. He felt obligated to give me what I wanted because he was my big brother. So he let me beat the crap out of him. The thing is, he's gentle. Fighting isn't for Brian. Same deal with competition or ambition. I teased him for being a chicken and a faggot. Who knows if he's ever had a girlfriend?—not me. He never complained when I rained verbal blows off his head. We loved each other and still do. Brian is genuine. There's not a false note in his body. Suddenly, I got powerful. That happened junior year of high school when I grew five inches and put on forty pounds of muscle. It was weird. I exploded into a totally different human being and next thing you know I was homecoming king and the homecoming queen wanted to take my virginity. Crazy as it seems, I was way too scared for that. I didn't want to lose whatever the magic was that had transformed my body by squirting it into a pretty girl. Can you *imagine*? *Me?* God's answer to *pulchritude*?"

We had many talks like that. Offstage and not in competition, Bubba and I were just like the rest of us—ordinary human beings.

Back to our story, however. About the only positive news I have about my separation-from-Rachel year of 1989 is that I had won every Big Arsenic fishing contest since 1983. I was still undefeated on the Río Grande. Imagine that! Small consolation, though. If I could have crowed like a rooster I would have, yet frankly I was too tired, all out of oomph, *épuisé*.

Life sucked.

Shortly before the 1989 Big Arsenic fishing encounter I rented a two-room apartment downtown and convalesced curled up on a floor mattress licking my wounds, my blood reeking of Verapamil, Quinaglute, and plenty of Coumadin. How did *that* happen? Every time I suffered a tachycardia or an atrial fib attack I performed the Valsalva maneuver. What's the Valsalva maneuver? It's a way to exit atrial fibrillation before it triggers the ventricular fib that will kill you. My new cardiologist had suggested the method to me.

You hold your breath and strain downward as if you are constipated and attempting to defecate. This stops your heart (and the arrhythmia) so the heart can restart again in normal sinus rhythm.

You hope.

. . .

"Marriage is not an easy project," Bubba agreed the night before our Big Arsenic showdown as we sipped Wild Turkey at my kitchen table with Yuri and Sharon Adair, who'd flown out from their new home (a loft in New York where Yuri had moved to be with her). This year's Bubba Babe, Melody Larson, was a hotshot stockbroker from Fort Worth who had once done eighteen months in a minimum security lockup for churning an account that belonged to Bunker Hunt. She had peroxide-blond hair; a hard, beautiful face; and a sardonic way of summing up her life. "Crime does pay," she told me, "as long as they only catch you for a third of what you stole. All the rest is gravy. I'm dating a guy right now who lives on a yacht in the Caymans."

She lit up a Gitane cigarette from France without asking anybody if it was okay to smoke.

Myself, I did not have a "date" for the weekend, I was still mourning Rachel. And, given the recent acceleration of my lifelong heart problems, I should not have been drinking whiskey, but so what? Pending divorce makes you suicidal. I wanted to crumple up and expire. How could I ever exorcise that woman from my heart?

Although Bubba was not suicidal, he said, "I think Tawanda and I may also be headed for splitsville, yet I'm leery because, despite the prenuptial, it's liable to cost me a bundle. I must've been snockered on absinthe when I asked her to walk the aisle. Already, Felicity Marie is bending the ears of a kiddie shrink three sessions a week. And Tawanda decided to quit drinking, go on a vegan diet, and I think she's having an affair with her acupuncturist from Calcutta. She even goes Sufi dancing with a bunch of diaper heads on Sundays. What happened suddenly to my life? I can't even locate any meat in my own mansion, I have to order out from Mr. Steak every night and they drive it over in a damn taxi that costs me thirty bucks."

"Poor widdle Bubba," Melody Larson said, patting sweat off his forehead with a folded napkin. "What can we do to assuage your anguish?" She ran her fingers through his magnificent curly locks. Bubba's hair was like the carefully coiffed "unruly" mop of that pumped-up Adonis, Fabio, who used to pose for the covers of romance paperbacks.

About his partner, Sharon Adair, Yuri said, "She keeps asking me to marry her, but I can't seem to call forth the gumption to do it. There's no doubt I love her, yet maybe all the positive tension would drain if I made her an honest woman. She earns double the salary I can command catching snook on a fly rod in the Everglades for *Gray's Sporting Journal*, which isn't a problem unless she begins to put on airs. 'Sharon,' I'm always telling her, 'work harder, earn more money so I can buy you things.'"

"Oh poor widdle Yuri," Sharon said. "What can we do to assuage *your* anguish?" She was a tall brunette who even in her stocking feet stood eight inches taller than Yuri in his black Wellingtons with two-inch Cuban heels. Sharon wore those big dark-rimmed glasses and, on first meeting, appeared studious and shy. Maybe even a wallflower. Turns out, however, that she had a wry sense of humor, indomitable stick-to-it-iveness, and was really smart.

"What about *my* anguish?" I asked.

Bubba, Yuri, Sharon, and Melody all looked over at me, and, in perfect unison, replied, "Your anguish can go screw itself."

Next day, despite the trauma and distraction of my pending divorce disaster, I left Yuri and Bubba in my dust. I can be indefatigable when rattled. First off, though, Yuri hauled ashore a sizeable brown trout, a lock for the biggest fish and an easy ten points. Then he pretty much stalled as I went into overdrive, and in the next three hours I enticed enough smaller trout from that swirling river to bury Bubba by a landslide, surpass Yuri's fat early lead by a slim margin, and notch my seventh straight Big Arsenic slam dunk, no need to bore you with the gory details. Let's just say the fish hopped out of the river into my burlap satchel like accommodating Shmoos from a Li'l Abner cartoon. If you are old enough to remember that strip, you will get the picture and the point.

Toward the end of the afternoon, each time I circled around Yuri to reach a higher pool I went "Beep! Beep!" like the Road Runner passing Wile E. Coyote. Exasperated, Yuri finally threw a rock at me, hollering, "You're an infant!"

Those words were our national anthem.

• • •

At the banquet that evening it was Bubba in a dour mood.

He still kept on his white Stetson, which he never removed indoors, not in a million years, not even if the president of the United States was in attendance.

"I don't understand why I can't beat him," he groused, dropping a maraschino cherry into his bourbon glass. "I'm a much better athlete. I'm rich. I pay millions in taxes. I'm a successful novelist. I'm handsome. I'm eleven years younger than him. I'm in perfect health. I have a beautiful wife and a bevy of girlfriends. I'm not a four-eyed preppy geek with asthma and a heart condition and a concave chest. So why can't I defeat him in this lousy fishing contest? *I can't even whip him yet on a tennis court.*"

Yuri lit his pipe, shook out the match, and inhaled. He said, "You can't whip him, Bubba, because his people came over on the Mayflower; his great-grandfather, times five, signed the Declaration of Independence for New York State; you're not a successful novelist, you only published one book; and you'll never win jack squat trying to cast flies wearing a cowboy hat."

"It's a *great* book," Bubba countered. "It sold twenty-six thousand copies in hardback, and the paperback is in its fifth printing."

"It sold *six* thousand copies in hardback," Yuri corrected him. "Then it showed up on the remainder tables at Marboro's for ninety-nine cents. And last I heard the paperback was being displayed on the juvenilia shelves at Barnes and Noble between Judy Blume and *Charlie and the Chocolate Factory.*"

"Boys, boys," Sharon Adair said. "Let's not get personal

here. And it's a wonderful book," she told Yuri. "You even said so yourself."

"What are you talkin' about?" he challenged her. "Who asked you to open your fat mouth?"

At that, Melody Larson went livid. "Who asked *you* to be such a boor?" she said. "You can't talk to people like that and get away with it."

"Wait a minute, you're way out of line, lady." Yuri leaned forward like a feisty bulldog. "We live in *New York*. We talk loud because that's how people from New York *communicate*. They are not feckless namby-pambies, they do not mince words. This woman is a shark. She can defend herself, do not be fooled by her timid demeanor. She isn't some kind of spoiled-rotten debutante from a gated Dallas suburb who was raised in taffeta and crinolines by a bunch of overweight Slim Pickenses who became autistic the second they couldn't talk about grain futures and pork bellies. This woman can cut your heart out with a put-down and nail it to your forehead with her sharp tongue. And don't you dare come back at me with some kind of feminist cant parroted from a PhD thesis by Ingrid Bengis or Germaine Greer because I'll bury you in rebuttal, okay?"

Melody Larson said, "Where I grew up most of the men were tall, thin, and weathered brown. They chewed Red Man or chain-smoked Camel cigarettes and drank too much whiskey and killed each other with knives in bar fights. They were sharecroppers, tenant farmers, field hands, virtual slaves. They toiled from birth until early death in the cotton fields, and their women, like my momma, had ten kids and washed all our clothes by hand, and cooked us grits and slabs of pork once a week if we were lucky. They also killed and butchered the pigs and stitched us dresses out of old flour sacks and made sure every damn one of us got to school on time and did our homework first thing off the bus so we could slop the hogs, feed the chickens and other livestock, bring in diapers off the line, and give bottles to the babies. I was raped three times by sixth grade, and my brothers Benjamin and David both died of the whooping cough because we couldn't afford to pay a doctor let alone hitch fifteen miles to the nearest hospital. All that aside, my momma and daddy taught us manners. I don't know who on God's green earth is German Greer or Inbred Benjy, but if you had walked into my town spouting your superior crap about taffeta and crinolines my daddy and his ilk would have fetched you up against a horse trough and given you a proper butt-fucking, Texas style, and don't think they would have hesitated for a minute. I've been to New York and my impression is that all those people can't run fast enough to escape themselves and the hell they've created to live in. So don't you talk to me about autism, big city sharks, or spoiled-rotten Dallas debutantes because I won't cut your throat with my sharp tongue, I'll use a real knife instead."

Yuri blinked.

Sharon was embarrassed. "I apologize for him," she said ruefully, placing her hand over Yuri's mouth. "If it's any consolation, his bark is a lot worse than his bite."

Yuri pushed her hand away. "It's not a *wonderful* book, Sharon." And to Bubba, Yuri said, "God strike me dead if I ever uttered such nonsense."

Before Bubba could respond, I said, "I think it's a cool novel. If he never writes another book at least he produced one fine work of art."

Yuri cast his disbelieving eyes toward me like a cat gearing up to pounce on a cockroach. "'A work of art?' Are you off your rocker? How much did he pay you to compare it to *The Southpaw* and *North Dallas Forty* when you blurbed it? Well, you know what I think? I think that someday you ought to wipe the shit off the tip of your nose."

I opened my mouth to speak, then stopped myself, I guess because maybe a little too much hostility gleamed from Yuri's eyes. In fact, his aggressive invective knocked me a trifle off-balance, like suddenly we weren't kidding around here playing the dozens. Briefly, I had flashbacks to all the negative critiques I'd laid upon Yuri's own tortured works. A cold lurch of discomfort caught in my stomach.

Bubba surprised all of us with an unexpected lack of brashness, an apparently uncalculated dab of virtuous humility. Perhaps even sincerity. "Yuri is right," he ventured. "It's just a run-of-the-mill potboiler I typed up for the hell of it. I can't pretend to have any depth in literary circles, but at least I had fun. Six months from now they'll shred it at the warehouse and use the strips, instead of Styrofoam peanuts, to fill their packing crates."

Yuri turned on Bubba. "Oh spare me from such twaddle, you affluent nincompoop." He sounded good-natured, even humorous now, an abrupt reversal of attitude. "Just for once be proud of something you did that indicates maybe your so-called talent hasn't completely ossified at a tender age."

Bubba's face transformed. Color popped into his cheeks, rosy colors, and his eyes lit up, though not in the way you'd think, revving his engines for a scathing riposte. They twinkled almost gratefully at Yuri's compliment, albeit left-handed, but all the same. And for a brief instant Bubba appeared to be honestly touched for all the right reasons. He did not know what to say, nor how to call forth an appropriate insult in response. It was a sight to behold and I realized our Texas buddy (just like yours truly), desired respect from Yuri, who was a harsh taskmaster. And wasn't that interesting?

Melody Larson exhaled a cloud of black tobacco smoke, saying, "The only thing ossified in Bubba is his choice of fishing buddies from back east."

When I cleared my throat to deflect her rancor, Yuri cast his eyes upon me, thrusting an emphatic finger in my direction. "Don't even *think* about it," he warned . . . and grinned at me as if there were deep and redemptive secrets we shared furtively between ourselves, truly intimate and profound understandings of women that separated us from the rest of humankind.

I have to admit that I harbored no clue to what was *really* going on. I got the impression that Sharon had the entire situation scoped to the nth degree. She rarely laughed, blustered, or shot off a wise-guy mouth, in fact she was quiet yet always seemed on top of any situation; she had *insight*.

Myself, I asked for, "More bourbon, please." And Melody Larson reached for the bottle, saying, "My pleasure."

Then she winked at Yuri. Impishly.

And Sharon—slightly—flinched.

Four

Jump-cut another four years to 1992, our tenth Big Arsenic contest, already, and yours truly is still undefeated—sound the trumpets! I had become invincible! Maybe there is another such victory streak in the annals of sporting America, though I personally am not aware of it. Yes, the heavyweight boxer Rocky Marciano was undefeated when his plane crashed. And during the 1980s Wayne Gretzky displayed similar bedazzlement on ice as a star of the Edmonton Oilers professional hockey team that I mentioned earlier. I won't include Tiger Woods here because he wasn't around at the start of our fishing challenge. However, let's not forget Sandy Koufax at his peak—the incandescent Hall-of-Fame southpaw.

Obviously, Bubba and Yuri were somewhat irked by then. Tough beans, although I certainly cannot pretend the Big Arsenic had been a cakewalk every autumn. Fact is, I had almost been snookered the previous year when weeks of rain muddied the water so badly that I captured only three small trout, yet one of them had taken the largest fish by half an inch over Bubba's lone contribution. Half an inch is as good as a mile, though you should have heard my despondent friends bellyaching. "That river beat me up," Yuri groused. "It stepped all over my blue suede shoes."

Bubba said, "You are the luckiest swindler I have ever gone up against."

What did I reply to them—?

"Poo-tee-weet."

At age fifty-two I retained in my possession the gaily painted wooden fish trophy from Puerto Vallarta, with my name (and the proper dates) now written nine times in Sharpie ink on its big yellow tail fin for all the world to admire. I displayed that trophy fish on the kitchen wall of my new house, purchased a year earlier, a prosaic 800-square-foot three-room adobe and cinderblock hovel with a leaky dirt roof located behind the Catholic church, with skunks under the floorboards and a toilet that barely flushed.

Why did I buy a house? Because I had lost my former digs and an acre of irrigated land to Rachel in our divorce. Then the landlady at my two-room rental apartment gave me the old heave-ho because I had rejected her amorous advances, a convoluted bummer that I prefer not to amplify here.

You mightn't believe this, but of late I had gone celibate hoping to somehow entice Rachel back for more. I'm not sure how to explain this implausible behavior. A harebrained measure, I know. What sort of tortured reasoning concludes that chastity equals seduction? Perhaps we had clashed with each other like two Vandal warriors brandishing broadswords and spiked iron maces attached to the end of chains, yet our perpetual bewildering contretemps had imbued me with a sexual delirium and emotional codependency that I know somewhere is defined as "anarchical burning love." And I could not quit myself of it. To be sure, the story of our Big Arsenic fishing contest bears no relationship to such a tyrannical obsession, hence I won't dwell on it. Nevertheless, I'd be remiss not to at least mention the problem in passing. Man does not live by fishing alone.

I found it impossible to whitewash Rachel from my mind. She was my Donnybrook, my Battle of the Bulge, my Dresden firestorm. I clumped about in a broody mode whistling melancholy dirges. Almost every weekend I casually drove by my old house longing to catch a glimpse of her out in the yard watering a hollyhock or perhaps in just her bra and panties hanging freshly laundered sheets upon the line. If by chance we happened to meet at the post office, I smiled at her, sickly no doubt, and Rachel nodded at me coolly as we chatted about the weather and whatnot. That woman possessed demonic restraint, fiendish indifference. For one, two, three years she had allowed absolutely no *connection* to pass between us. Who knows how she accomplished that? I myself ached for her so badly I'm surprised I did not suddenly haul off and whack her with a right uppercut in front of Uncle Sam's postal clerks and all their patrons.

My older daughter, Stephanie, said, "Give it up, old man. You're running in place and will never win the race." My younger daughter, Naomi, added, "Pop, you should go to a proctologist and have your head examined." My girls think they are funny. It's a genetic blemish inherited from guess who? Their mother, Gretchen, wisely withheld comment on my situation. There was no need for her to verbally dig my grave since I could accomplish that very well myself. Gretchen and I maintain a distant but civil relationship, all for the sake of our girls.

Anyway, enough already. I purchased the cheap shack that required all my savings left after the divorce and put me in dreadful debt. Rachel, the once-radical journalist cum special ed teacher cum museum-diorama artist, had now become a successful local therapist and drug counselor, raking in the shekels hand over fist. Misery loves clinical sympathy. Understand, I'm not hollering foul play. You can't blame your life on anyone else. As soon as Rachel swiftly earned a master's in social work she obtained certification and licenses in family and addiction counseling, then aced all the relevant national and state exams, whereupon bipolar heroin addicts and suicidal mortgage brokers began knocking down her door for help. She also led popular group sessions for Adult Children of Alcoholics. The local grapevine informed me that Rachel excelled at marriage counseling, anger management, child abuse, battered women, and transformational guidance, whatever that is. She was on the board of Community Against Violence, aiding a wide range of disparate personalities who were dearly helped by her insightful empathy and wisdom. Strange as it seems, my second ex had a real gift. How could I compete with that?

Not for ages had I spotted Rachel around town with another guy. This fact sort of gave me hope. Could she be suffering too? On one occasion I bumped into her at Smith's accompanied by a bearded young stud pushing her shopping cart, but he turned out to be her youngest gill-netting son from Alaska, name of Willard. When Willard shook my hand he almost broke every bone in it. The other son, Maynard, was doing time in a Cordova jail for firing an AR-15 at a rival salmon boat infringing on his territory. Both lads were a couple of hotheads like their mom.

Professionally, I hasten to add, I too had arisen from my ashes. My personal life aside, I can often pass for a creative, hardworking, reliable guy. I had published another novel; I was polishing a new screenplay. The novel was called *A Eulogy for My Funeral.* My narrator, a recently tenured young college professor of biology, understands that global warming is already destroying the earth, there's an enormous ozone hole over Antarctica, and climax capitalist consumption offers an untenable future for humankind and all other life systems on earth. In short, we are facing planetary extinction. When the professor begins teaching these facts to his students, the administration warns him to back off because his subjective politics are destroying his academic and scientific credibility, objectivity, neutrality. Jeremy Napier (my protagonist) refuses to kowtow to the president, the dean, and the Committee for Academic Fair Play. One day he falls in love with a French professor at the same school who happens to be a Parisian divorcée with attractively kinky sexual proclivities. Needless to say, she and Jeremy take up half a chapter in which their erotic hanky-panky is described at great length and with a most colorful vocabulary, one of my great faults as a writer (and, I suppose, also as a human being). I cannot resist scribbling borderline pornography and calling it great art (me and Erica Jong!). It sells books but usually offends the critics, who seem impervious to the literary allure of ample bosoms, stiletto heels, and almost Shakespearean foreplay in a novel about "the end of the earth." If I can live with the dichotomy I don't know why they can't.

The kicker in my novel is that the French professor is actually an administration stool pigeon who snitches on Jeremy, accusing him of rape. I won't tell you what happens next—go out and buy the book.

The film I was polishing took place within the Amazon jungle's Kayapo Indian reserve on the Xingu River where the Brazilian government planned to build a huge hydroelectric dam with funds obtained from a World Bank loan. My job was to rewrite the screenplay imbuing the Kayapo principals with a touching depth of character. Warner Brothers was financing development, and I had read a half-dozen books to research the Kayapos and also watched a series of documentaries about first contact of Europeans with native Amazonian tribes. At the film's payoff, Kayapo representatives at a Manaus courtroom actually succeeded in making the Kayapos' case and defeating the dam. I feel it was an important film and a great script, so of course it went into turnaround and thence into mothballs on the shelves of some studio's morgue, a pity. But I was proud of my work and happy to earn the bread, because even as a bottom-feeder on the Hollywood food chain I was, comparatively, rolling in bucks.

Keep in mind, however, that I was scrambling to cough up out-of-state college tuition fees for my daughter Naomi, I had to make three car payments each month and also meet exorbitant family health insurance costs, and there was a significant back-taxes debt to the IRS. Therefore, despite my literary "success," I was still frantically treading water to keep my head *above* the water. Commie ideals are great unless you were born middle-class and want to die middle-class, whatever the cost. So sue me. What's my excuse? I live in *America*.

· · ·

"I don't believe this grubby place," Bubba said. "It's a roach hotel."

"It's what I can afford." I jutted my jaw at him.

"When I was twenty-one I lived better than this in South Philly, one block from the projects," Yuri said.

I ignored them—Mr. Smug. "I own the Big Arsenic trophy," I said, pointing to it on my kitchen wall. And for solace, after all those bumps in my rocky road, I could peruse my growing album of Big Arsenic snapshots that gave me a self-satisfied chuckle to look at. Pictures of me bussing lunkers or holding our fishing trophy aloft as if it were the silver Wimbledon platter. I reconnoitered photographs of drinking bourbon with my pals, and of we three aging reprobates posing at the Big Arsenic Springs trailhead with our rod-case erections upthrust toward the camera, laughing like silly redneck bubbas. Nobody could have predicted the grim destiny that lay in store for me (and, coincidentally, for us). How could they when I had on display so many point-and-shoot images of inebriated party girls seated on my lap at the annual banquets hugging me with great élan as they pretended to be awed by my prowess with an implement of ichthyoid destruction?

And you can bet my fingers were always raised in a V sign: *Look on my fish, ye mighty, and despair.*

On the negative side, I'll admit my heart problems had worsened. A prolapsed mitral valve was growing flabbier, and no cardiologist could properly track down the source of my now chronic atrial fibrillation. Holter monitors had proved ineffective, echocardiograms useless, too. Earlier that year, after I got lucky with an old flame who resurfaced after her third divorce, I required cardioversion with the paddles at Holy Cross Hospital *after* they gave me an adrenaline shot to curb an asthma attack.

"You're falling apart," Bubba said gleefully. The day before he and I had clashed on a public tennis court, resuming our oft-interrupted rivalry, and—surprise!—he thoroughly cleaned my clock. No longer a "lucky pissant," I scarcely knew what hit me. Bubba destroyed me with pantywaist popcorn lobs whenever I rushed the net. He'd never before swatted high, curving floaters that forced me repeatedly to backpedal. His patty-cake returns drove me nuts, kept me off-balance, ruined the rhythm of my game. What had prompted *that* strategy? In the past, once Bubba learned to play, he had aggressively walloped the ball, hitting it too far, too high, too low (into the net), and double-faulting his blazing serves. In a power game, even after he became relatively competent, I could stave him off because he was catering to *my* strengths. Yet over the past year some Machiavelli had taught him to *be* Machiavelli, and his new style upset my applecart. When I viciously whacked his powder-puff returns it was *me* who drove them into the net or beyond the rear service line. Bubba's tennis game

77

had become the opposite of his personality, and I fell right into the trap, losing in straight sets, 7–5, 7–5. Close, but no cigar.

When we met at the net to shake hands, Bubba said, "You will *never* take another match off me in your life you uncoordinated, bumbling ragdoll of a human being. This is just a prelude to the Annual Big Arsenic twenty-four hours away. Get used to it, you Milquetoast. I'm going to take the high ground, now, and not even rub this in. When I win the contest tomorrow, however, I'm going to crucify you with my celebration."

Then he hugged me, saying, "I love you, bro. For an old derelict you've still got a lot of mettle." It didn't even register that he might be being snide; I felt too much like crying. Losing in *any* way, shape, or form to Bubba was intolerable. I'm not talking about kissing good-bye to my cliché manhood, that sort of testosterone-driven flummery, I'm not that shallow. I'm referring to a way deeper, most likely existential, angst.

For example, watching Bubba leave the tennis court ahead of me jaw-popping and cowboy-walking like a monster brown bear from Kamchatka *almost* drove me insane. And he knew it, too. In Bubba's high-stakes and high-anxiety world the meek did *not* inherit this earth.

• • •

On other fronts, in a fit of pique (and compassionate bravado) Yuri had now married his partner, Sharon Adair, who had remained in New York this year working to pay the rent while Yuri flew out alone two weeks early so that we could fish up and down the Río Grande to get in fighting shape. Some trails into the gorge were so steep we needed to pull ourselves uphill at dusk, grabbing one sage bush after another. Suicide Slide was composed of loose gravel in a V-shaped chute out of which it was nearly impossible to climb. "You're killin' me," Yuri complained. "I'm too old for this!" We also hunted blue grouse up high in Saloz Canyon, following ancient logging roads that circled the foothills above Pot Creek and the Río Chiquito. We had seen two bears, twenty elk, five porcupines, a ferruginous hawk, and a very rare boreal owl. Then I transported Yuri to Holy Cross Hospital for a treadmill test because *he* was experiencing chest pains. Nothing to worry about, the doctors said, "It's only indigestion."

"I wonder about that," Yuri mused after we arrived home and he had swallowed a fistful of Tums. "I honestly don't feel so great. I've got a left bundle branch that's scarred from an incident three years ago."

"You *what*? Are you *kidding*? You never told me about that."

"I don't tell you everything, my man. You get maudlin so fast it makes your own ears whistle."

"You had a *heart* attack?"

"It was an incident. A minor episode. Forget about it. I can't stand cloying."

"So why'd you bring it up?"

He looked at me like the Godfather deciding whether I needed to be popped or not.

I couldn't forget about it, though. To be honest, now that I had a new piece of information, Yuri did not look unambiguously healthy. His face seemed pallid and drained yet also too flush. He was sweating and maybe a little scared. You might even say he seemed vulnerable. But it was Yuri's style, his shtick, his persona *never* to seem vulnerable. Tough as nails. Bullet proof. Don't let the Yahoos catch you napping. It was an affectation he and Bubba had in common.

I added, "We're still young. We must have walked ten miles today."

Yuri dipped a lit match against fresh tobacco in his pipe. "'Live fast, die young, have a good lookin' corpse,'" he said. "Who wrote that?"

"Willard Motley. *Knock On Any Door.*"

"Where did he die?"

"Down in Mexico."

"How old was he?"

"Fifty-three."

Yuri said, "My age exactly. I wish Priscilla Endicott hadn't gotten that abortion long ago. She was the first woman I ever actually cared for. If you hadn't come up with the dough maybe she wouldn't have done it and I'd have a kid out there somewhere today."

That surprised me. Yuri had not mentioned Priscilla since the night a gifted and conscientious doctor, a woman whose name was never revealed to us, had performed the abortion after-hours in a certified clinic somewhere on the Upper East Side of Manhattan.

"When I offered the money you told me to give it to her," I blurted.

Yuri touched my shoulder reassuringly. "I know, I know.

Calm down. I didn't want the kid either. We were both young. We had lives to lead. It made sense."

"I wonder whatever happened to her?" I said.

Yuri shrugged. "She cut me off like an unpaid electric bill in the slums. I wonder if she ever wonders what happened to me?"

"We'll never know, I guess."

"*I* know what happened to me," he said.

"No you don't," I replied quickly. "We're still young and in the process of becoming what we're going to be."

Yuri started to mount his high horse, yet paused with just one foot raised to the stirrup and asked me with a sort of gentle, almost admiring scornfulness, "Tell me, my friend—how much longer do you intend to wear those rose-colored glasses?"

Awkwardly, I said, "I didn't know you cared."

Yuri smiled. "Forget about it. I am not a sentimental person."

"You're a *good* person," I said.

He replied with a snicker, "Well, then, there, now."

And Bubba was still hitched to Tawanda . . . barely. Sadly, their home life was a mess. Shot full of Wellbutrin and Zoloft, Felicity Marie now occupied her own condo above the stables, next door to the harpsichord recital den. Her mom had quit being a vegan, retired from the aromatherapy chain, and now worked full-time training for marathons. Believe it or not, she'd actually finished among the top thirty runners of her age group in Boston *and* New York. "And next month she's gonna do a triathlon in Hawaii," Bubba said. "Anymore, we're never home at the same time. We have sex once every six months if I'm lucky. Her personal trainer is a former Olympic weight lifter who won a bronze medal in Munich."

At least business was booming for Bubba. A month earlier he had opened another Racket Ranch in Salt Lake City where all the canned music piped into the weight and exercise rooms was recorded off of records by the Mormon Tabernacle Choir. "Members *love* it," Bubba swore. "A stroke of *genius* on my part. And there's a special sauna yurt outside for bigamists."

I remarked silently that he did not appear so all-fired tremendous himself. Bubba's face was a bit puffy, right on the cusp of bloated, and I had the impression he'd been drinking heavily. Stress, I suppose, combined with lack of exercise. It's not easy being a mogul.

Denise Lefkowitz, that year's Bubba Babe, I recall fondly. She was a tarty nugget of eye candy from Las Vegas whom Bubba had met at a sales powwow out there last spring and flown to New Mexico expressly for 1992's Big Arsenic blowout. She called Bubba her Goy Toy. "This man is so *special*," she cooed, squeezing Bubba's arm with phony consternation. Then, obviously well coached, she ordered, "Make a bicep, sweetie. Show these tenderfeet who's the real king."

Bubba rolled up his shirtsleeve and flexed, exposing a bicep still the size of a cantaloupe. Denise licked the tip of her index finger and touched it to the muscle, mouthing a sizzle sound—"*Ssssst!*"—and jerking the finger away as if she had tapped a burning coal.

"Oh my, what a humdinger!"

We laughed. Denise was a fancy blackjack dealer in

her hometown and I confess that I envied Bubba his partners in crime at every Big Arsenic banquet and his immaculately clear conscience. Yet occasionally I almost felt sorry for him and his imploding married life because I had a sense that Tawanda meant a lot more to Bubba then he'd ever let on. And, whatever her adolescent drawbacks, he surely did love Felicity Marie. "She's the apple of my heart."

"Eye," Yuri corrected. "The apple of your *eye.*"

"Get thee behind me, Faulkner," Bubba growled.

· · ·

On game day, 1992, Bubba drove us north in his ostentatious brand-new SUV. As usual, it was only Yuri and me along for the ride because Denise and my date, Adele Wiggins, had remained behind to shop, visit art galleries, and regale each other with lurid anecdotes about the foolish toddlers who'd obligingly coughed for their all-expenses-paid weekend in enchanting New Mexico. Naturally, we enjoyed our regular eats and condiments, washing down the traditional baloney and swiss cheese sandwiches with Heineken beer and fistfuls of Pringles potato chips, Real Heart Food for Real Men.

A few miles out of town Bubba announced, "They're finally going to make a movie of my novel. Polygram and Universal are putting up the bread, Ridley Scott will direct, and Burt Reynolds will play the coach. Loni Anderson is the hooker."

Yuri yawned. "Don't bother me with your tripe," he said. "I haven't the patience for it."

Bubba turned to me. "What's the matter with your

little pink friend?" he asked. "You two commies remind me of Elmer Fudd and Bugs Bunny. I earn twenty-five thousand dollars a year for an option on *The Obnoxious Noseguard,* and the minute they exercise that option I'll receive a cashier's check for a hundred and twenty-six thousand dollars. And a little after that, soon as they commence principal photography, they have to fork over two and a half percent of the shooting budget up to another hundred thousand smackers. Suck on that, you Lilliputians."

"His lips are moving," Yuri said, "but no intelligible sound is coming out."

Understand, Yuri did not begrudge Bubba all his Racket Ranch loot. However, Bubba's book and movie success grated big-time for obvious reasons. Yuri himself had commenced a new novel after the last one fizzled despite countless revisions. The final draft of the old book that he sent to me was so belabored it read like an open coffin in a mortuary with no mourners in attendance and lugubrious organ music leaking from the background.

"I don't know what happened to that manuscript," Yuri said now, truly depressed. Bubba was fifty yards ahead of us on the Big Arsenic trail, racing to rig up and start the ball rolling even before we reached the river. "I was so in love with it for so long and then all the love dried up," Yuri continued. "I'd kill myself if I had the guts."

I said, "No you wouldn't. You have a good life. You travel places. This year you've already fished Argentina and Montana, and for tarpon in the Florida Keys. And you wrote great articles about all of it for very popular magazines. You have a million readers."

"I write 'great articles?'" Yuri stared directly into my eyes with his upper lip raised in an almost frightening sneer; I sensed he was on the verge of tears. "You know what I hate?" he said.

"No, what?"

"I hate writing about fish for magazines I wouldn't use to wipe my ass on if I could help it."

We gazed at each other. Yuri had dark eyes, that handsome curved nose and tough lips, and a beard stubble, and his hair was slicked back, always perfectly combed. Even down in the gorge not a hair was ever out of place. And under his fishing vest he wore his usual black T-shirt. His body was small and compact, although over the last few years he'd developed a curious little pot belly. His tightly pegged Levi's hung very snug, and he wore cheap, low-cut sneakers, no socks; the sneakers were falling apart.

I loved Yuri. He was my alter ego, my doppelganger, my ghetto brother. He had made me tough, giving me credibility, through his friendship, with a world my upbringing had known nothing about. I had learned so much about life and literature and *attitude* from Yuri. And about culture, foreign movies, slang. His defiant stubbornness and uncompromising work ethic aimed at creating great art permeated my soul. His anger and ferocious hatred of mundanity gave me inspiration. To me, that bravura was extra heroic because I myself lacked his courage, I lacked his self-destructive integrity.

"I'm sorry," I said.

"I scorn your pity," he answered.

. . .

Then we were lined along the river braced to commence yet another Big Arsenic fracas, each one of us placed at a different pool fifty yards north of the Little Arsenic Springs *comme d'habitude.* I can picture the scene, as they say, as if it was only yesterday. Bubba is wearing his white cowboy hat, high-end polarized sunglasses, an Orvis fishing vest, neatly perma-pressed pleated Docker's trousers, and expensive athletic brothel creepers.

Yuri has on a Phillies baseball cap, aviator shades, his wicker creel, and the rest of the outfit I described above.

Myself, I look appropriately grubby in my sun-bleached John Deere cap, my tattered vest over a JCPenney's work shirt, grimy chinos that I never washed and used exclusively for fishing, and pathetic tennis shoes from Walmart. Call the wardrobe my impersonation of Red Skelton's "Freddie the Freeloader." No, I've never been a clotheshorse, but my shabby ensembles for our fishing contest were deliberately exaggerated to throw them off. "Look, I'm a klutz, relax, don't take me seriously."

And by the time they woke up they were history.

In those barbaric times, Bubba and I carried very un-PC green plastic mesh landing nets with plaid bungee strands on the handles clipped to the O rings on top of the backs of our vests. Nowadays, they throw you in jail for using a net like that which might damage the delicate scales of a Noble Trout. Today I wouldn't hurt a flea, God forbid, even if it carried the plague virus, for fear of contributing to species extinction or the greenhouse effect. Yet back then we could not have cared less about harming any gilled vertebrate that might have qualified as points in our fishing contest. Nobody had promised those creatures a rose garden.

Too, during the early stages of our duels we utilized cheap Shakespeare fiberglass rods and reels. Six weight lines, eight-and-a-half-foot rods, which were about right for a rough-and-tumble stream like the Río Grande. Personally, I have never been a fan of equipment. I'm a reverse snob that way, skittish about overindulgence and lopsided expertise, a reaction to the elitism of my prep-school education that was subsequently torpedoed by my descent into Marxist doublespeak. Later, Yuri became fascinated by the quality stuff laid on him by tackle manufacturers whether or not his magazine articles plugged their products. His communist beliefs never got in the way of pocketing the vigorish when it was offered. And one year Bubba visited my town bearing gifts for Yuri and me, lovely graphite rods, top of the industry, with double-tapered Cortland floating lines on mega-special reels. I did not fancy the reels; they were too small and too dainty for the Río Grande. Personally, I preferred a Pflueger Medalist big enough so that a traditional line only filled half the spool's capacity. To be specific, my Medalist was a #1498 as advertised in the Cabela's catalogue, a veritable howitzer. I was not interested in backing on that reel, either, because I never tackled a stretch where you could let a trout run much farther than ten feet before it got tangled up in enough crap to finance a sewage plant.

Those quibbles aside, Bubba's graphite rods were cool.

Basically, however, we had a rule of thumb that good

equipment was wasted on the Río Grande because we almost always fell into the boulders and smashed it.

. . .

During our tenth duel in 1992 I experienced my greatest triumph on the Río Grande and also suffered my most egregious setback (prior to the ultimate tragedy a few years later that ended our kerfuffle for good). Around 6:00 p.m. I climbed upriver to where Yuri was quartering my favorite pool. I was disappointed he had arrived there first. I called it the Niagara Pool because of a pinch at the tail blocked by rocks that formed a dam creating an eight-foot waterfall on the downstream side. White water at the wide head of the pool evened out to deep water swerving under a channel cut into solid rock on the west side. The center of the hole was dark green and probably twelve feet deep. To access the dam you were required to negotiate over slabs of protruding rock on a ledge covered by damp algae, which gave a nice upstream cast to the undercut rock wall and a fast drift down. I knew that if I finished the downstream drift by pulling my flies directly across the front of the dam I could coax big fish up from below where they liked to congregate.

"Hey, Yuri, you're in the wrong place," I called. "There's nothing but minnows at the head of this pool."

He turned and glared at me, irritated. His pipe was clenched between his teeth.

"Come here where I am and cast over a little above the dam," I suggested. "You'll catch a whopper on the drift."

His answer? "Shut up. I know what I'm doin'. I earn a *living* catching fish."

"Do you mind if I try this part, then?" I asked. I couldn't bear to see him spoil the hole.

"Knock yourself out," he said.

Stepping carefully over the wet ledge, I stopped at a pinnacle of stone higher than my head that stood at the east side of the dam. On a small declivity in the boulder, even with my eyes, clung an odd green clump of moss, a domed nest fashioned by water ouzels—dipper birds. I set myself, casting upriver and across to the rock wall. My flies were tugged under by fast water and I felt the strike instantly, a big fish, with no need to set the hook. It sprang out of the water, catching Yuri's attention, and then a larger trout banged my dropper fly and hooked itself. There was a splashing of glittery pinkish rainbow silver as I panicked and cut loose an exclamation. Both fish swooped over the dam as I yanked out a big loop of line and flung it up over the rock with the ouzel nest on it. Then I scrambled backward, holding my rod as high as I could as I circled clumsily through shallow water to reach a lower level. Yuri staggered after me shouting, "Oh my God! Oh my God!" He was excited.

Below the waterfall ran a deep channel for twenty feet flanked by rocks and more rocks, no quiet water. I had line coiling free all over tarnation as I hurried to keep up with the fish while cranking my reel to recapture line.

Incredibly, when my rig swept from the deep channel into a shallower place of rocks and gravel beds, both rainbows were still attached. I sideswipe-swung my rod backward, holding the butt with both hands, almost breaking the rod tip and heaving both fish clear of tumultuous froth onto a gravel bed where I swiftly netted one in a foot of water, the wrong one, the eighteen-inch rainbow attached to the dropper fly. This meant I could not net the sixteen-inch guy on the tail fly below. So I pounced. When you've lost composure and complete control of the situation, that's what you always do. You pounce. The tail fish flopped through my grasping hands until I managed to flip it up-line into the net. And I had them both. "Holy mackerel!"

I couldn't breathe. I was kneeling in shallow water, astonished by my good fortune, fumbling through a vest pocket for my Albuterol inhaler. I looked up. Yuri stood over me exclaiming repeatedly, "Oh my God!" He had his net unlatched from the O ring on his vest and extended toward me ready to help.

I grinned at him, and the first thing I thought to utter was, "*That's* how you fish that pool."

He flung his net at me and the wooden frame almost broke my nose.

• • •

Yuri never apologized and I can't say I blamed him. Hiking out of the gorge that evening was no fun for me because I felt worse than exhausted. I knew in advance I had shellacked them both by at least fifteen points, yet my heart was bouncing around like a ball made of Flubber trapped inside a squash court. My legs ached so badly from lack of oxygen that I stopped repeatedly to rest. My nose had swelled to the size of a pomegranate. At one point I sat down midtrail and started crying from exhaustion and from apprehension about my erratic heartbeat. The heart hopped and lurched and raced, and I felt queasy and faint. A neck artery pulsed wildly; I touched it and withdrew my fingertips in shock. Because of the dark Yuri and Bubba could not see my face, thank God. I did the Valsalva maneuver and drank cold water until my heart finally clicked back into normal sinus rhythm. When it did that I experienced a sensation similar to an orgasm flooding all the muscles and organs of my body. I shivered gratefully.

My pals were so concerned about my well-being that while I was seated on the trail struggling not to die they had been arguing about Thomas Pynchon, deliberately ignoring me.

"I just finished reading *Gravity's Rainbow*," Bubba said. "He's the greatest writer in America. Comparable to James Joyce."

Yuri gesticulated scornfully. "What do you know about Thomas Pynchon? You can't even read Beatrice Potter or A. A. Milne. And Pynchon is an inflated windbag, a poseur, a faker. What he creates is duplicitous erudition, intellectual schmaltz. Pulp fiction. Written in self-conscious idiosyncratic vernacular emblematic of total cognitive dissonance. I'm not saying that out of envy or because, like you, I haven't read the man. I'm not that callow a fool. I enjoyed Benny Profane in *V.* hunting those alligators through the Gotham sewers. I actually thought *The Crying of Lot 49* was a decent little piece of irony. And I read every stinkin', paranoid, grotesque, mathematically questionable word in *Gravity's Rainbow*, because you owe a writer that, whoever he is, present company excepted. But you know something? Pynchon couldn't even take a dump in James Joyce's outhouse. He ain't even close to a third-rate Franz Kafka or Hemingway full of tall daiquiris on a bad day in Havana. He's too clever for his own britches, and I can't stand his apocalyptic nihilism. If you have to work that hard to read a writer he had better *tell* you something. 'The greatest writer in America?' Bubba, you've got less brains than a newt on a dissecting table in a high school biology lab."

Bubba shot back, "You're so smart, what's the name of the main character in *Gravity's Rainbow*?"

"Who wants to know?"

"I do."

"You're beneath me," Yuri said. He made a brushing-off movement with the back of one hand. "Go away, your ignorance is stultifying. There's a thousand characters in that overblown piece of obtuse blather."

"Name one," Bubba insisted.

"Up yours."

"How about Slothrop?" Bubba leaned in for the kill. "Does he by any chance ring a bell? Who's the person he screws on the *Anubis*? Do you even know what the *Anubis* is?"

Yuri bent his head to better regard Bubba with disparaging quizzicality. "What are you *talking* about, you moron?"

Bubba was on a roll. "The *Anubis* is a boat. A ferry boat. And on board they're having an orgy. The second girl he screws is an underage child and her name is Bianca. Her mother is grooming her for the movies. Oh, excuse me— you don't remember?"

Yuri stuck his face up close to Bubba's snout. "What does that prove? That you read the bent-over pages in a library book because they deal with kiddie porn?"

"What's the name of the main female character in *The Crying of Lot 49*?" Bubba fired at point-blank range, both barrels.

Slightly nonplussed, Yuri said, "I don't remember. I rarely wallow in bad literature's irrelevant details."

"Oedipa Maas," Bubba crowed gleefully. "Man, you are a pedantic ignoramus. When was Thomas Pynchon born?"

Yuri regarded that imbecile with astonishment. "Who on earth gives a shit?"

"May 8, 1937, in Glen Cove, Long Island, New York!" Bubba spit out ecstatically. "You don't know *fuck-all* about Thomas Pynchon." He did a little Ali-shuffle dance and a double fist-pumping exercise at waist level.

The veins in Yuri's temples bulged out as if he'd just begun chewing a blisteringly hot jalapeño chile pepper. He sputtered, "You wanna read a *real* writer? You wanna read somebody who makes Thomas Pynchon look like an escargot on a cracked platter in a cheap French restaurant? You wanna brag about reading somebody who's actually intellectually *complicated*? Read the Jorge Luis Borges story 'The Aleph,' you simpleton, then get back to me with some substance in your literary remarks. Remember that—'The Aleph.' I repeat: it's a short story by Jorge. Luis. Borges. You can read it in fifteen minutes and then *think* about it for the rest of your life."

"I feel sick," I mumbled. "I think I'm dying."

Bubba, feeling superior and in command, said, "Don't be hysterical. Take a deep breath, concentrate, and quit hyperventilating." Then, turning to Yuri, he added, "*Fuck* your Aleph."

"It's my heart," I groaned. "And my nose is killing me."

Yuri settled down on the trail beside me. Bubba sat down on the other side placing his hand on my shoulder.

Yuri said, "You deserve that schnoz. Your arrogance is intolerable for a mediocre scrivener who writes like Ernest Hemingway wearing a Japanese kimono and Birkenstock sandals. You're an asshole."

"Amen to that," Bubba agreed. "Pride goeth before a fall," he added. "That's how the Roman Empire, the Greeks, the Sumerians, and the Ottomans bit the dust."

"But what can we do for you?" Yuri said, scowling venomously at Bubba. "Ask and it shall be granted."

"I don't know. Maybe you bozos could help me onto my feet so we can make tracks out of here."

They both stood up. Yuri gripped me under my right arm, Bubba under my left, and they helped tug me upright. They held onto each elbow while I teetered and struggled for better balance. I wavered, really unsteady; my chest hurt, a dull, heavy pain.

"Don't die," Bubba said cautiously, worried about me now. "We've got your back. We'll get you out of here, I promise."

Yuri said, "American literature would never forgive us if we let you croak."

Bubba agreed. "And what would Hollywood say?"

God, I was tired. I wished we could clomp offstage, swab away the greasepaint with cold cream and Kleenex, and become normal people for a while. Their sarcasm was all in jest, of course, although I sort of grasped that maybe it wasn't as harmless as I would have liked.

Gently, however, they guided me up to the rim.

. . .

Heading north that night along the deserted Wild River road we had to stop once, letting a porcupine waddle across the macadam. Next, a solitary deer smack dab in our way stared into the headlights until we beeped it off. A half-mile farther on a swooping great horned owl almost hit the windshield. Yikes. Yuri said, "I don't *believe* you landed both those fish."

"It's genetic," I muttered. "I inherited my prowess directly from God."

"Oh spare me," Bubba said. "You inherited *shit* from God. You're as phony as a three-dollar bill. You pretend to have a goody-goody left-wing social conscience but in actuality you're a male chauvinist pig who treats women (and also writes about them) with abysmal patronizing and abusive emotional prejudice, and even though you earn hundreds of thousands of dollars working on Hollywood blaxploitation movies, you hide all the money in secret savings accounts, live outwardly like a bum, and tell everybody that all the flicks you're writing are feminist epics about social justice, racial equality, liberation from wage slavery, and environmental protection. Bull hockey, squared. Even my brother, Brian, who's the most trusting soul on earth—he gives *everybody* the benefit of the doubt—would see right through you to your rotten hypocritical core in the first five minutes! If Billy Graham had a nephew with Down syndrome *and* Asperger's, you would be him. There's not an honest bone in your body. I can't stand your Puritanical New England superiority complex that masquerades all over the place like a humble, self-effacing Christer when underneath you're more redneck and intolerant than Hank Williams Jr. and David Duke. At least I'm not a two-faced Yankee egomaniac who constantly pretends to be what he's not. God wouldn't give you the time of day, and Saint Peter would arrest you for even approaching the pearly gates. You're a *blithering* asshole."

Yuri cast Bubba a perplexed glance that was almost admiring.

Back home, Adele Wiggins and Bubba's date, Denise, were already so tipsy they could barely stand up; lamb chops percolated under the broiler flames. My heartbeat was quieter, yet I still felt out of sorts. At the unveiling, Yuri and Bubba glared at my pile of lunkers, but what could they say except, "Curses, foiled again!" When Denise sat on my lap to pose for a picture, she teased, "Marry me, and let's run away to Morocco." I was holding crushed ice wrapped in a washcloth against my nose. Adele plopped onto my thighs and touched her lips against my ear, whispering a bit of impudent country music doggerel—"Oh what a man, what a man, what a man my *man* is." Per our custom, I posed for more portraits proudly displaying the painted wooden trophy fish from Puerto Vallarta. And after that, for the tenth year in a row, I printed my name and the date with a Sharpie pen on its big yellow tail, finishing off my John Hancock with a feeble attempt at a flourish.

Then I ducked because Bubba had aimed the third bottle of Möet et Chandon at me as he popped the cork—it missed. "You lose again," I said, managing a raspy cackle. *Jesus*, I had a headache.

Yuri grumped, "You fish like you write, it's all blind luck."

"I can't seem to help myself," I mumbled. "I have a magic touch."

However, that night in bed with Adele I was miserable. Too much booze, too much everything. My head and my face ached and Adele could not stop talking about Tibet, about her abusive stepdad, about her manic-depressive stepsister, about her trip to Sri Lanka, about her Jungian analyst, about her monthly colonic enemas, and about her desire to flee corporate America, go back to school, and earn a degree in anthropology. I finally lost my temper. "At least you haven't been kidnapped and raped by extraterrestrials and then went to a shrink who specializes in sexual abuse experienced during alien abductions."

Adele didn't think that was funny. She lay beside me buzzing with malignant electricity while I breathed stertorously through my swollen beak. When I finally apologized for being such an insensitive oaf, she said, "You three guys are so *puerile*."

"It's only for one day a year," I reasoned.

"That's one day too many for my tastes," she replied. "I'm sorry I ever agreed to visit you this weekend. You're a first-rate asshole."

"That's three times today already," I griped. "Can't you use an alternate derogative?"

But then she caught me entirely off guard by asking

plaintively, "Do you like me at all or am I just another one of your vapid party dolls?"

"I like you," I said, awfully groggy and itching for reconciliation. "I think you're a sweetheart."

"Oh, thanks for all your enthusiasm," she replied. "At least stop being so hateful and make love with me like you almost mean it, okay? I am not a nobody. Let's pretend for a minute that we're real people instead of cartoon characters."

Yes, I had decided to break my morbid vow of celibacy because Rachel had totally ignored me since God knows when. My abstinence had gotten me nowhere. And I was *horny*. All the same, this felt like it would be adultery. That said, Adele and I kissed each other and embraced, making love with amiable consideration, and then fell asleep in each other's arms. Or, rather, Adele conked out right away. I found it impossible to nod off because Rachel occupied my guilty mind. I couldn't keep her at bay. Scrambled thoughts tormented me. For example, if I challenged her about some issue her eyes would begin to glitter and she'd smile like a serial killer ready to pounce. I feared that look even as it gave me a hard-on. Rachel made me feel *alive*. When we played Scrabble occasionally at night after dinner she would remain a paragon of even-keeled attentiveness unless I had built an insurmountable lead as we ran out of wooden letters, at which point she'd casually poke the Scrabble board off our table, saying, "Whoops." That was a signal for me to forget the score and attack her, go crazy flailing away on the parquet, then shower together before falling exhausted into bed.

Even then I'd dream of Rachel, always Rachel, high-octane Rachel with her explosive imagination, fiery temper, and contagious laughter. Rachel derisively ordered me to fuck her faster, harder, longer, better, crazier, and then suddenly rolled away from me and jumped off the bed and threw up her arms hollering, "What's the *matter* with you? Why are you so *intractable*?"

"I *love* you!" I cried out in my dreams.

"Your 'love' is the enemy of my freedom!" she answered.

Five

You think you are going to be young forever, then suddenly you're not. I won't bore you with the electrifying details of how I managed to sweep the annual Big Arsenic rivalry in 1993, 1994, and 1995. Who can explain my obscene domination and all the depraved ways a person can reign over a ludicrous fishing tournament? The fact is I lucked out in countless arcane circumstances and even captured the 1994 crown when nobody scored a single qualifying trout, hence the gaily painted wooden trophy remained with me, the champ.

Nonetheless, fatigue was setting in. By the time of our fourteenth Annual Big Arsenic Fishing Contest (on September 29, 1996) Yuri and I were both a trifle long in the tooth, and even Bubba was evolving toward middle-age. He had turned forty-five last February, had a bit of a paunch, wattles beneath the chin. His recent knee surgery was holding up okay, considering. "I'm as tough as the Dallas Cowboys," he boasted. They had won three of the last four Super Bowls. "My manhood is still magnificent," Bubba added. He touched his fingertips to his fly, making the "*Sssst!*" sound as if the zipper was piping hot, and jerked back his "burnt" fingertips in mock alarm.

Per tradition, on the night before our tussle we lolled around my kitchen table with the girls nibbling on smoked oysters and drinking Wild Turkey 101. All our fly boxes were out; I had tied three leaders for Bubba; Yuri was greasing his reel with graphite lubricant squeezed from a thumb-sized tube. It was a pleasant scene until Bubba said, "By the way, they're actually on location at last for my movie, boys, what do you think of that? New producers, new studio, new writers, different director. When they finally exercised the option I put that one hundred and twenty-six Ks in the bank. Chicken feed. When they started principle photography I made another hundred thou, free money, I deserve it. Then they hired me to be a script consultant at twenty-five hundred a week—pocket change, spending cash. I'm so rich the Pope sends me a Christmas card, Paul Newman invited me to his box at Daytona, and Tanya Tucker thinks I'm cute."

"Tanya Tucker wears combat boots," Yuri said.

No question, Bubba was rich. All the same, his pending divorce from Tawanda did not sound like a barrel of laughs. They were still negotiating after too many years. Aside from thirteen Racket Ranches (including the just-opened Aloha Ranch on Maui where hula-dancing classes accompanied the Jazzercise workouts around a heated pineapple-shaped exercise pool) and his meager holdings in my town, Bubba now owned four luxury hotels, two Cineplexes, three Nevada brothels, and a marina on Lake Powell, Arizona. Far as I could discern, his equity overshadowed his debt by about twenty million dollars. Or thirty million, what did I know? Yet although his prenuptial agreement had been designed by three of the most sagacious Colorado barristers, Tawanda had recently hired herself a pedigreed shyster of uncommon ingenuity who was becoming a pain in the ass.

"I made a bad mistake when I offered her a couple million up front, tax free, and promised to buy her an eight-hundred-K house if she wouldn't hire a lawyer to defend her interests," Bubba said as his date for our contest, a poor little rich girl from Aspen named Marjorie Kittredge, poured him another bourbon on the rocks and plopped a maraschino cherry on top, the official cocktail of the Annual Big Arsenic Fishing Contest. "I threw in the Suburban, the Mercedes, and three-thousand-a-month child support when Felicity Marie is living with her," Bubba continued. "But the devious crone showed my generous proposal to a female lawbooks who told her it was an insult. She said any man who would do that deserved to be ripped apart, so she took the divorce on a contingency basis claiming if she couldn't bag her ten million plus three thousand alimony a month for life, plus 'very generous' child support, plus full ownership of our current digs, she'd make up the difference to her out of her own pocket. Those people never quit, do they? What's the problem if you have six of them buried up to their necks in sand? *Not enough sand.*"

Grinning, Yuri leaned forward puffing on his pipe. He teased, "You're a contemptible arriviste, Bubba. A codfish aristocrat. You deserve to get taken to the cleaners, you obnoxious noseguard. Give me Tawanda's phone number.

I'll call her up and hand her enough scuttlebutt to hang you fifty times over from a yardarm."

"What advice would you give me if you were my divorce lawyer?" Bubba asked Yuri's wife, Sharon Adair, who by now did have her name on the shingle of the family law practice where she had worked for years.

"Remove your hat in the courtroom," Sharon said. "And for God's sake don't take the stand on your own behalf." Then she asked, "Seriously?"

"Seriously."

Sharon pulled no punches. She took off her glasses, assayed Bubba for a moment like a prosecuting attorney lining up the ducks for an attack, then crisply, without any hesitation, let him have it. Sharon was taller than anyone else in the room, and the assertiveness of her voice made her seem smarter than all of us, too.

"You don't have a leg to stand on," she began. "I doubt the prenuptial will protect you. From what you've revealed they can probably prove she signed under duress, inebriation, false pretenses, moral turpitude. It sounds as if her lawyer will hire PIs to track down every hidden asset you've accumulated and then demand a square deal or she'll notify the IRS, a blackmail threat you should acknowledge—nobody likes to be up shit creek without a paddle. Since her lawyer is operating on a contingency basis she has the motivation to expose every shady scheme you ever concocted, including anonymous bank accounts in Nauru and on Bimini, or wherever you keep them. Gleefully, she will further destroy your character by tracking down all the seedy affairs you've conducted over the past fifteen years with trollops eager to snitch on you as rightfully they should. That's not cause for a priori assumption of guilt, but you don't want to go there. I assume if you fail to strike a compromise by conceding to her at least a third of the estate that's been put on record during your marriage, you'll be depositioned so aggressively that you'll wish you'd never been born. My advice is to shell out half the assets on your books, keep quiet about everything below the line, and be grateful if that calls off her dogs. Otherwise, she can tear you apart in court until all your secrets are revealed and then you'll end up behind bars. Maybe she's bright enough not to push it that far, because she might wind up without a nickel into the bargain. But you'd be mincemeat. So swallow your pride, give her the moon, and be grateful to escape with your private parts intact. At heart, you're a criminal. Everybody on the bench and in the jury box will know that. Act accordingly."

Incredulous, Bubba glanced over at Yuri as he gestured toward Sharon. "Who is this person?" he asked. "You're *married* to her?"

"Listen up," Yuri advised. "She wants to help you."

Bubba performed an instantaneous sea change that startled me. Startled all of us, frankly. His good-old-boy belligerent facade collapsed like a deer shot through the heart and was replaced by the forlorn mien of a beleaguered man dangling at the end of his rope.

He said, "You're right, I need help. I lie in bed every night wondering, 'How the hell did I wind up here?' If you people think it's easy governing an empire you ought to try it sometime. I spend twenty-eight hours a day running figures through my brain: profit and loss, staff salaries, managers robbing me blind, legal confrontations with contractors, subcontractors, city hall, town planning and building codes, construction costs, bank loans and collateral, equity spreadsheets, updates, replacements, tax rates, tax shelters, tax payments, IRS audits, rents and leases, equipment malfunctions and manufacturers' wholesale discrepancies, weekly HIV tests for the hookers, roundups of the illegal alien janitors and kitchen workers, bias against women in the workplace, lawsuits because there was a fungus in the hot tubs, egomaniacal workout instructors, landscaping 'artists,' county health regulations in the kitchens and cafeterias, garbage disposal contracts, health insurance and maternity leave, and trying to divorce my wife without losing it all. I must have twenty lawyers on my payroll, and three overseers who I trust more than God himself just quit. I'm flummoxed. I wish I could blow it all off, become a reclusive on a Kauaian avocado ranch, and write another book."

"About what?" Yuri asked.

"About my mom and dad. A memoir. They never had much of anything. My dad killed himself doing menial labor for cruel bosses, but he never complained. Years ago I bought them a two-bedroom ranch-style house with AC on the North Side in a tony little subdivision near Buddy Holly Memorial Park, nothing fancy. I added sprinklers to the lawn. Later, I wanted to upscale them to a better neighborhood, adding a pool and a hot tub, a billiard room in the basement, and a three-car garage, but they refused. They were happy. Every weekend my mom bakes Dad a pecan pie and they invite my brother, Brian, over for a pork roast, black-eyed peas, and cornbread muffins. Brian does the yard work around their house on weekends; I gave them a seven-horsepower Lawn-Boy. Weekdays, Brian sells used Fords and Chevy pickups, and GMC three-quarter-ton flatbeds at the American Motors Preused Lot, which is the biggest in north Texas. He's the only honest used-car salesman you'll ever meet. The thing is, it works for Brian. People instinctively trust him. And they are right to do that. He wouldn't ever cheat you on a deal. Nobody can take advantage of him, either, because he understands exactly what is fair and never exaggerates or underestimates. Nope, he ain't an intellectual and he never went to college or read Plato, but he's got more humility and integrity than I could ever dream of. Except for me, my family is upstanding, ordinary decent people. Mom's a great cook. They'd all much rather eat meatloaf and gravy than chateaubriand. The only liquor Dad ever drinks is Budweiser beer. Brian avoids booze. Mom's a teetotaler, she doesn't believe God intended for you to imbibe spirits. I once tried to teach Dad about good wine but he stared at the bottles like they'd come from outer space. My folks were born humble people and they'll die humble people. Proud and unassuming. According to Orville and Purcine, the nicest gift I ever bought for them is two plots in the Benediction of Jesus Cemetery in South Lubbock right across from the Christ Almighty Baptist Bible College. I love my mom and dad."

"Don't we all," Yuri said.

"I mean seriously," Bubba said. "Don't fuck around with my parents. Or with my brother."

"Touchy touchy," Yuri remarked.

"I'll touch *you*," Bubba warned, and he *was* serious.

• • •

Yuri was only three months older than me, yet by now he looked really peaked. Peakèd. His dark hair was turning gray. His skin was pale and blotched and his crooked yellow teeth had a couple more gaps. "Dental insurance?" he scoffed. "In this backward country? What's that? I bank sixteen grand per annum paddling canoes on the Green River for *Sports Afield*, but there aren't any medical benefits or workmen's comp. I earned a master's in creative writing from Johns Hopkins, so what's wrong with this picture? I never planned to be a tragedy, but I've written five serious novels now that are putrefying in basement boxes three blocks north of Canal Street while you two schmendricks are laughing all the way to the bank."

He added, "There's no point in takin' care of your teeth."

Sharon said, "I love him anyway. Beauty is only skin deep. His heart is made of gold."

Yuri squinted at her, then surprisingly clasped one of her hands. "She 'loves' me," he said, almost gently. "Who would've thunk it? Somehow, I landed in high cotton. I pulled a lever and beat the house odds with three peaches in a row."

Sharon appeared a trifle frayed around the gills herself, her brunette locks fading to gray, her crow's feet expanding exponentially. She and Yuri had been married for four years and together for thirteen. It seemed they had finally mellowed, though they still bickered and sniped too much. In private, Yuri told me that although he truly loved her, he was plagued by his other demons and often hunkered off in corners like a petulant troll reading essays by Montaigne. Why

Montaigne? "Because I *like* Montaigne," he said thoughtfully. "I feel like I'm also wandering through the countryside during an outbreak of plague. Increasingly, I feel lonely. I wanted my life to be better than this. I thought I could be an artist."

I had said, "You *are* an artist. I've learned more from you than from anybody."

And he had replied, "Is that a compliment, or are you trashing me?"

Sharon, tired of custody battles and family property wars, now piped up with, "I'd like to retire next week."

Yuri flung aloft his arms: *"Over my dead body!"*

But then he hopped into her lap and held onto her large frame like a little boy at Christmas with Santa Claus. And when they kissed you could tell they really meant it.

. . .

Me, I had celebrated my fifty-sixth birthday two months earlier at the end of July and I could display a scar from my throat to my bellybutton to prove it. Don't ask, I'll tell. Although this is embarrassing, I may as well fess up. I had already been remarried and redivorced (for the third time in my life) since our 1992 Big Arsenic fishing contest. Sounds loopy? It's true. Who did I marry? Three guesses, the first two don't count. That's right. Rachel and I were drawn back together like Richard Burton and Elizabeth Taylor, like Diego Rivera and Frida Kahlo, like the Dodgers and the cursed Yankees long ago during their 1950s World Series clashes. Suddenly, she and I had collided again and couldn't keep our mitts off each other.

It started this way. I phoned her office to make an appointment for counseling. She asked, "What's the problem?" I said, "I'm depressed, I can't get motivated, I'm lethargic, I'm drinking too much, I'm in a tailspin, I need help." "You and everyone else," she retorted coldly. "See a shrink, get some Prozac." "I need help from *you*," I wheedled. Rachel harrumphed, "You're out of your mind. I am a professional. I'm wise to you." I pleaded, "But you're the only person who understands me." "Yes, unfortunately, that's true," she agreed. "And for that reason I wouldn't touch you, in my office, with a ten-foot pole." I assured her, "I won't break any of your precious client/therapist rules." She pointed out, "The fact that we're even having this phone conversation is compromising my client/therapist rules." Then, who knows why—her demons? my demons? ghastly serendipity?—but she made an appointment with me.

We had not spoken intimately for several years. Yet five minutes into our session we began groping each other against her desk, and twenty minutes later we finished our unexpected collision in a noisy clatter of rapturous exclamations while grappling on the office shag rug, thus breaking all her rules.

"You son of a bitch!" she hissed.

"I've missed you terribly!" I gasped.

"You don't deserve me!" she snarled.

"I can't live without you!" I groaned.

"Okay," Rachel said, abruptly as calm as the eye of a hurricane, "but I don't want to live together. You crowd me and you're out. I need my own space."

"Me too," I echoed euphorically, proving that human

emotional complexities (and libidos) are unfathomable. Question: How can it be that I had mysteriously cajoled what I wanted from this upscale, morally committed, rational, responsible, respectable, and even-keeled feminist icon? Answer: You can never tell a person by their public persona.

A week later we completed our blood tests, purchased the marriage certificate, and said "I do" before a magistrate judge. It was just her, me, the judge, and his doddering secretary who'd been with him for three decades. We had conscripted two witnesses from the lobby, the chubby guard who checked everybody through a metal detector and an off-duty cop waiting to bail out his ex-son-in-law jailed for failure to pay eight months of back child support. Rachel had dressed up for the occasion in jogger Nikes and ankle socks, aluminum-colored exercise shorts, and a T-shirt with a Smokey Bear logo. We planned to go running afterward. The judge said, "Ma'am, could you please remove your gum?" Rachel had woven her blond hair into a long braid and she had a good tan. I could picture her as one of the players on America's World Cup women's soccer team—healthy, athletic, and with the sharply alert eyes of a peregrine falcon. You had to really keep a close watch on Rachel to surprise her looking drowsy, usually only around the time of her period (which was ending with menopause) or after sex. Otherwise, she appeared ten years younger and ferociously alive and arresting, like a maid who could have passed for Joan of Arc centuries ago. Intimidating, regal, sensual . . . and, somewhere in there—part of her great seductive charm—alluringly childlike. Shirley

Temple meets Jaqueline Bisset. Rachel was always catching me off guard, that being part of her personality gimmick. I never knew, when we woke up together, if she'd nestle snugly against me needing sex, or hop out of bed, grab a cup of coffee and a glazed donut, and be out the kitchen door before I even realized that her feet had hit the floor.

Over the next three years our frenzied intellectual brawling led to emotional exhaustion, extreme jealousy, finally preordained betrayal, and down we twirled again spectacularly in flames. During that hysterical epoch I almost died of endocarditis, then I segued into congestive heart failure, suffered open-heart surgery (they stitched an annuloplasty ring to my mitral valve), and next, for good measure, I underwent a double hernia operation and got divorced once more.

"Never again!" Rachel and I pledged in unison to each other as the divorce papers were being signed, and we sealed our vows with a final spasm of carnal excess. At least this time around no houses and very little money changed hands.

My older daughter, Stephanie, now happily married and the mother of a comely infant, Callie, studied her wristwatch and predicted, "I bet you two start screwing each other again in two years, seven months, sixteen days, five hours, and thirty-two minutes." My younger daughter, Naomi, now a college premed student aiming to be a pediatrician, said, "Dollars to donuts, Pop, that your relationship with Rachel is just beginning."

"What *is* it with you and women?" Yuri asked.

"I am hopelessly in love with her," I protested. "You

know that. I can't erase her off my mind. I am obsessed by her imagination, her emotional fervor, her energy, her intellectual dexterity. The sex with her is like a wonderful car crash that never ends, the vehicle just rolls over and over down a—"

"What can she possibly see in you?" Bubba interrupted.

"I am a respectable writer. I have an uproarious sense of humor. Politically, I support all the right causes, both environmental and social. I love the outdoors, the alpine ridgetops, the Río Grande gorge, our high-desert sagebrush mesas. I love movies and literature. I listen to Amy Goodman on NPR. At home I do dishes and vacuum carpets, take the laundry to Peralta's, fix the roof and prune the apple tree. I'm civil to her boys when they come to visit us from Alaska and pass endless boring days chewing the rag about seals robbing sockeye from their gill nets while Indian fishing rights are keelhauling their vocations. I don't eat too much, I keep in shape, and in bed I'm like an indefatigable conjugal warrior who's not afraid to manifest his feminine side. And furthermore—"

"Jesus, you're a lost cause," Yuri said. "An emotionally arrested person, just like your literature. The epitome of gauche. When will you learn that infatuation is not intimacy even if it lasts for a decade? You have to travel beyond the need for perpetual thrill. You must calm down and prepare for the long haul. Love is not a hundred-yard dash, it's a marathon. Relationships are hard work. Sex is not all it's cracked up to be. Read *Portnoy's Complaint*. Or maybe even take the plunge and plow through *Anna Karenina*. It wouldn't hurt you to open a Flaubert tome, either. Or maybe sink your teeth into *Hedda Gabler* or Jane Austen. Women are way more than Dolly Parton and Jayne Mansfield. Did you ever read Strindberg or *The Kreutzer Sonata*? You might even approach a novel by Edith Wharton. Or take a break from the paucity of your intellectual range and crack a tract by Hegel, try some of his dialectical laws on for size, then push on to Engels and Marx with their materialistic view of history which you claim to espouse even though you've never read *Das Kapital* or *The Origin of the Family, Private Property, and the State.* Bottom line, you are a shallow dilettante. An amateur lothario. You even write pop fiction like a dilettante, with little or no emotional depth. You describe the surface of things with a fancy-schmancy vocabulary, but you never investigate *underneath.* I pity your offspring their genetic roots."

"Thank you," I said.

"Don't thank me. I'm only a third-rate adjunct professor in the University of Relationship Advice."

Bubba chimed in with, "If we ran him up a flagpole, nobody would salute him."

"*I* would salute him," Bubba's girl, Marjorie Kittredge, offered. "I think you fellows are being mean."

• • •

All the next day during our fishing contest I had trouble walking along the Río Grande shore, my balance seriously out of whack. When I had almost died of endocarditis two years earlier they had given me four weeks of an IV antibiotic called Gentamicin through a Heparin lock in my throat feeding directly to my heart. While that quelled the strep infection inside the heart, the side effects rubbed out the vestibular reflexes of my inner ears. Hence all my balance was now exclusively visual. The condition causes the disequilibrium of oscillopsia and has no cure. My tennis days were over. And lack of coordination would hound me into the grave. Learn to live with the ataxia, dude. I seemed to be learning the hard way.

I stumbled often and could not wrestle myself onto large boulders anymore or jump off of them. No way could I hopscotch across the river on the stones as I had formerly. My prospects had seriously diminished with age and its attendant calamities, and it all seemed to have happened in the blink of an eye. Life is quick. Nevertheless, I report (in all humility) that I did land a fourteen-inch brown trout, and then a couple of hefty rainbows that I wrenched ashore like a stevedore. Once you know how to ride a bicycle you never forget.

Two-thirds of the way to the Big Arsenic Springs there's a large curve on the river that we called Killer Bend. A wide swath of basalt boulders had tumbled down to the water, big boulders, some of them six or eight feet high. A stately old juniper tree grew from the rocky jumble forty feet above the shoreline. Rushing water had sanded and smoothed the boulders around and below it, pounding through black basalt to form archways and other architectural marvels. You had to crab carefully through the carnage to reach patches of fishable water, but it was good lunker territory *if* you could horse them out.

Bubba came galloping by ahead of me and veered left to a stretch I favored, maneuvering swiftly through the rocks to arrive at the best pool first. That ticked me off and I cursed him for commandeering the water I wanted. Used to be I was a regular ballerina compared to Bubba, and now look at me, a near quadriplegic worming through no-man's-land. I resented Bubba for still being agile.

After that bend in the river the canyon opened up and the Río Grande quieted, level for a moment; the shoreline had grassy sandbars and easier walking. As I was plugging along feeling pooped and belligerent, I heard a scream and turned around. From high atop a boulder Yuri waved his arms at me, so I doubled back.

"It's Bubba. Something happened."

I'll say.

My curse had worked.

Our wealthy clown had misjudged a leap onto a slime-covered rock and skidded into another cracked garble of soaked basalt. When I arrived at the scene he was seated slumped over on a stone surrounded by gushing water, too stunned to move or even glance up at us. He had saved his cowboy hat and was clutching it against his chest. Gingerly, Yuri and I rappelled through the boulders until we reached the spot. We had to bite our lips not to laugh because Bubba appeared so totally *destroyed*. Picture Mussolini hanging upside down, or Hitler at the end in his bunker.

"Are you okay?" I yelled.

Bubba shook his head, he was pale, his lips blue, he could not budge. I tried to maneuver toward his position without falling in, a challenge. Managing to approach close enough, I could tap his shoulder by leaning over a narrow cascade of violent water coursing between two monster slabs of stone. Amid them a waterlogged tree trunk was lodged at a goofy angle.

"Give me your other hand," I said. "Let's get you safe on shore. Pass the hat to Yuri."

"Nobody touches my hat." Bubba settled the Stetson onto his head, then gave me his hand. His rod lay across his lap, the tippet section broken. His reel was also smashed. Bubba leaned toward me, bending downward as I tugged him forward, and he jockeyed over the hissing spindrift onto my rock as I leveraged backward, almost taking a plunge. Yuri was straddling the rocks behind Bubba, and he deftly captured Bubba's rod before it went into the water, no mean feat. I hauled my friend toward me and then he muttered, "I can do it myself."

Painfully, Bubba worked his way to shore over the slippery basalt and, at each of his steps, I cringed, resisting an urge to steady him, thereby losing my own balance. He gave me the heebie-jeebies. *We're pushing this macho crap too far*, I thought. *Time for an allee-allee-in-come-free.*

On shore my friend sank to his knees among saw grasses, wild milkweed, and some bleached juniper driftwood. "Let's go home," I said when I had reached solid ground myself. "The Big Arsenic is called on account of injury. Nobody wins, nobody loses. It's a long walk out of here."

"It ain't dark," Bubba said, rising slowly to his feet, wincing as he straightened up. "We always fish until dark. I'm ready. Let me at that river."

He bent backward and twisted stiffly from side to side, testing, shaking his wrists to loosen them. I pointed out,

"Your rod is broken, Bubba. Give it up. We'll call it a tie and come back next year."

"I can fish with it. I can whip you both with a broken rod. You did it to us once, didn't you? Get out some Band-Aids so you can make me a splint. And I'll need the extra reel in your pack."

That was the straw that broke the camel's back—not mine, Yuri's. He had come ashore with Bubba's broken rod and was standing beside me marveling at the hubris of our fellow piscator.

"Don't give him the reel," Yuri said. "Hang onto your Band-Aids. I'm fed up with him dissing you all the time when he himself has the mental capacity of a dust mite. When I read his stupid novel you know what I thought? I thought it was one big cliché from start to finish. It's so derivative and sophomoric and jejune that it embarrassed me. I've read better fiction in the *Reader's Digest* at the St. Vincent's emergency room. That book is like a Keane painting of big-eyed clowns with teardrops on their fat painted cheeks. They should've published it with a velveteen fuchsia jacket and taped a pink lollipop on the back, then sent you on the rubber chicken circuit to plug it in the Catskills."

Where had *that* invective come from? Bubba had published *The Obnoxious Noseguard* ten years ago, and in Yuri it still rankled? Bubba cocked his head, scrutinizing Yuri, wondering was he serious or was this just more of the dozens?

To set him straight, Yuri shook his pipe in Bubba's face. "You know something, you pompous rich schnorrer? You don't have an original thought in your empty head. If I had published anything even remotely resembling your piece of noxious teenybopper bubblegum I would have apologized to all my friends and family members and then jumped off the Brooklyn Bridge. When I take a shit my turds are shaped like the state of Texas."

Okay, Bubba had gotten the picture. "Wait a minute," he said. "Hold your horses." And he rent the air with his typical magniloquence. "I made over two hundred thousand dollars when they exercised the option on my book and started principal photography!" he yelled. "You haven't earned mouse doots from all that self-conscious drivel you scribble, you loser!"

"I'm happy for you," Yuri yelled back at him. "To my way of thinking they can't pay you enough to honor your lack of talent!"

They stopped. I thought Yuri would hit him, but he didn't. He stared at Bubba, though, and Bubba glared right back. The veins in Yuri's temples were standing out, his face was incarnadine from wrath, and his forehead was covered by large sweat droplets.

Then Bubba shouted, "You couldn't sell a book even if your own mother was the publisher!"

Give him credit, Yuri did not blink. They confronted each other for a long time like a couple of elderly bighorn rams on a ridgeline at thirteen thousand feet during the rut in December. And their face-off scared me because it looked as if they truly hated each other. This wasn't just the dozens. They both seemed one inch shy of mortal combat. Most people would have pegged their money to Bubba because he was younger and bigger and still quite a physical specimen, with a neck like a baobab. But I would have bet on Yuri because he was a fierce little mongoose who had enough anger and resentment to fuel the gravitational pull of a black hole.

Then I experienced one of those revelations that pumps ice into your heart and makes you sweat simultaneously. I wondered if it was possible that both of them hated *me*. Like, why wouldn't they? I had published a bunch of books and written screenplays and been married and divorced three times to and from a couple of glamorous women, I had two cool kids, I had won some awards. And I had knocked the stuffings out of them on the Río Grande for fourteen years in a row, including this year when my gunnysack was so heavy I might have to hire a guy with a donkey to cart it out of the gorge for me. Also, I'd teased and ridiculed both of them for failing to conquer me, I had bullied them with a low-key braggadocio disguised by an affable false humility that, if you thought about it (which I never had until now), was despicable. And of a sudden I became overwhelmed by waves of guilt and shame for winning our fishing contest fourteen years in a row, for taking it all so damn *seriously*. In fact, I ran the entire narrative of our annual fishing competition through my brain like a drowning man does with his lungs full of water, and as I did I pondered this: What sort of needy, small-minded, insecure fanatic immersed in low self-esteem had had to prevail every year, for Pete's sake? In retrospect, why did I never kick back long enough just to enjoy the show and revel in the glory of the gorge? *What kind of inhuman aberration was I, anyway?*

Yuri said, "Bubba, I'm going to tell you something. Do me a favor and prick up your ears. Before the Holocaust my father was a respected jeweler in a tiny Polish village called Wyszków north of Warsaw. By the time he made it to the United States after the war he had a number tattooed on his wrist. A miracle that he survived. He met my mother on Compton Avenue in North Philly and spent the rest of his life on a bench repairing cheap watches for Macy's because that's the only weekly paycheck he could muster in America. He was a virtuoso on the violin and once entertained ambitions to play for the Philadelphia Orchestra, but reality would not allow that dream. My father and Rudolf Serkin were pals. After supper on Friday nights we all reconnoitered in the living room, my mother, my father, my brother, Sherman, and we listened to classical music. We sat very quietly and paid attention because my father said it was *important*. And we respected his opinions. Nobody ever lit a candle in our household on Friday night; my parents were not observant Jews. They both carried a card in the Communist party, praise their misbegotten souls. For a long time they could not fully perceive Stalin's evil. My mother sewed fabric in a garment shop for twenty-eight years. She was skilled at a machine. Nobody in my family believed in an afterlife, or that you could earn even a modest living without working your fingers down to nubs. But we believed in music. We believed you could take a break from the dislocations and tragedies of daily life by listening to Rubinstein on a Friday evening, or maybe Toscanini conduct. Yehudi Menuhin on violin. It was a peaceful vacation from reality. It's the way my mother and father recharged themselves and I learned that trick from them. I've always understood that it's important to suspend belief every now and then, ease up, de-escalate, and let music or something comparable enter your soul. Are you following me?"

Bubba said, "My name is Yon Yonson, I live in Wisconsin, I work in the lumber camps there . . ."

Yuri extended his right arm toward the Río Grande as if introducing Bubba to the river. "Every year," he said, "I come out west to visit our friend here, and we walk around in the mountains, we fish the smaller streams, we sit at a table and drink bourbon and clean our equipment. And once a year we join up with you and hike down here to the Big River and have ourselves a raucous fishing contest. I savor the ballyhoo. I enjoy being on this portion of the Río Grande. But in order to fully appreciate the day I have to ignore the way things really are, which is that humankind is destroying the planet. The industrial revolution, carbon dioxide in the atmosphere, ozone holes, greenhouse effect, the collapsing nation states of Africa, the social injustice and unequal distribution of wealth on earth, overpopulation. I needn't elaborate on the litany. Even you must have a clue in that hollowed-out musk melon that balances precariously on top of your shoulders. Climax capitalism is a voracious predator, let's leave it at that. And when I contemplate the Río Grande what I really see are cascading waters filled with toxic molecules due to acid rain, to nitrogen fertilizers and pesticides and herbicides generated by potato farmers up north in the San Luis Valley, to sewage plant overflows all along the canyon, to mercury carried out of the high mountains through the erosion spawned by old logging roads built almost a century ago, and so forth. Every year the New Mexico Department of Game and Fish publishes a report on the contamination of this state's water, its rivers, lakes, little streams. I ask them to send it to me because I research all my potential articles thoroughly even if I never write them. And that report cautions me to consume only four trout caught from this river over a three-week period. Probably my stats are off but you get the picture. And if I was pregnant I shouldn't eat *any* fish from *any* of the lakes and streams in New Mexico because that might deform my fetus."

Bubba said, "Mares eat oats and does eat oats and little lambs eat ivy. Little kids'll eat ivy too."

Yuri said, "The reality of this river is that it's a sump pump for pollution. Not a pestilent wasteland yet, though headed in that direction. The entire world is headed in that direction. Look at these waters. Ain't they beautiful? I love this river. It's a privilege to fish it every year. It's a gas to have rollicking fun with you two illiterate clodhoppers down here each autumn. But I have to suspend reality in order to enjoy myself during the Big Arsenic contest. Forget about climate change, global warming, sewage effluent, and fertilizer pollution. I can do that. We can all do that, it's a built-in genetic protective device for survival. Otherwise we would all commit suicide. However, it disturbs me when your unenlightened yakking torpedoes my contemplative afternoon. Hence, what I'm trying to say, in the most civilized manner I can summon, is 'Why don't you ever shut the fuck up so I can have a good time while we're fishing?' Quit being Daddy Warbucks for a few hours in order to relish the fact that we three people are able to live in a time when all of this around us isn't yet totally ravaged, despoiled, decimated. Am I making sense? Listen to the music of these fabled waters. And stop. Ruining. My. Day. Just join me and Genghis Khan here and enjoy the fact that we're *alive*. Is that too much to ask?"

Bubba raised his arms and mockingly began to play an elaborate imaginary violin as he said, "Your insults are like a gentle caress."

Yuri couldn't help himself, he began to sputter . . . and then he laughed. What are you gonna do faced with a former Red Raider noseguard from a family lineage shackled by premature senility? And something changed, like the barometer did a flip and began rising because the storm was over. And shortly Bubba laughed. Soon both of them were laughing until, overwhelmed by relief, I commenced giggling myself. Whew. All three of us had dodged another bullet. And after that I dug a spare reel from my knapsack and also reached for the Band-Aids.

"Forget about it." Bubba waved me off. "You're right. We need to go home." He seemed almost repentant, possibly even contrite. Yuri could reach Bubba where most other angels feared to tread. "Nobody wins, nobody loses," Bubba concluded. And to me he said, "You're still the champ, you cocksucker. Wait'll next year."

• • •

We climbed out of the canyon that night proceeding slowly in deference to limping Bubba. Too, we were still jittery, walking on eggshells. "Damn this river," Bubba moaned.

"Why do we do this? What's the matter with us? I hate this vile gorge."

"Me too," I said. Yet before I could stop myself I had added, "I'm exhausted from always winning."

Bubba said, "Your days are numbered. I'm going to take out a full page ad in the *New York Times* the minute I win this contest. You are one pathetic human being."

"*Bath*etic," Yuri corrected. "Bathetic with a 'b.'"

On a break, we tilted our heads back to admire the Milky Way, but Yuri and I could only identify the Big Dipper and the evening star until Bubba said, "There's Pegasus . . . and Aquarius . . . and Sagittarius—"

"I never learned the constellations," Yuri interrupted. "It's a flaw in my education. However, I've read Copernicus and Galileo and Kepler and Tycho Brahe. I said Tycho Brahe. Do either of you illiterate peasants know who Tycho Brahe was? No? I'm shocked. He was a sixteenth-century Danish nobleman. He was kidnapped from his cradle. His nose was sliced off in a duel. He had a prosthetic nose made of an alloy of gold and silver. He invented the quantitative measurement of astronomical phenomena. He built incredible quadrants to precisely observe the firmament. Kepler called him the 'Phoenix of Astronomy.' Tycho had a fool for a pet, a dwarf called Jepp who sat jabbering under the dinner table during banquets. Tycho was an arrogant genius and a pig to his servants, but he mapped the sky with more precision than anybody else had done. He was famous for discovering a new star in 1572. That's right, I said 1572. Later, Tycho exiled himself from Denmark and met Kepler in Prague, and after Tycho died, Kepler inherited his mantle.

Tycho Brahe's final words were '*Ne frusta vixisse videar.*' Does anybody know what that means? No? It means, 'Let me not seem to have lived in vain.'"

Bubba said, "And over there you can see Andromeda and Perseus. And a little to the left is Auriga."

Yuri did not go after the bait again. And neither did I. So Bubba clammed up, too. We all piped down—a miracle. Maybe, for once, we were honestly too drained to keep yammering. Or maybe we had decided to wear the consoling cape of friendship silently, with no abrasive badinage for once. In any case, we continued climbing out of the canyon, gasping and grunting, same old, same old. It was warm, with a trace of vanilla scent on the air when we passed the Vanilla Tree. I stared at the ground, trying to keep my balance, which was difficult. Yuri fell behind me and Bubba pushed ahead, then I stopped so Yuri could catch up. When he reached me he paused, puffing, bewailing the steep trail. After he'd sort of caught his breath, I said, "You never told me all those things about your father."

Yuri gave his right hand a dismissive flick to one side. "I lied," he said. "Forgive me. I made it all up. My father was born in America. He never went to war, and never met Rudolf Serkin or played the violin, either. He graduated from Rutgers and sold life insurance for Aetna. I just wanted Bubba to quit flapping his lips."

Then Yuri gazed up at the glittery foam of the Milky Way that half-filled the sky. He looked haggard yet full of spunk despite himself.

"Of all the things I do," he murmured, "of all the difficult places I travel, in Newfoundland, rural Maine, down in the Caribbean writing my articles, this is the toughest." He paused, catching more breath. "Every year that I come out here you try to kill me on this river, or bushwhacking for grouse on game trails in the mountains." He canvassed the stars a few more seconds, then lowered his gaze to my eyes. "It's a beautiful world," he said. "Don't we have fun?"

"Yeah, we have fun."

"Thank you for giving me this country over the years," he said quietly. "It has blessed my life. And so has Bubba Baxter. I agree with you—his book is wonderful. But don't ever tell him that, his ego is out of control. And, just for the record, you ain't such a bad writer, either."

Yuri pinched my cheek affectionately, then turned and plodded uphill again. I remained stationary a moment longer, startled by his compliment, watching as he faded into the darkness. Pretty soon he had vanished. I shifted my attention to the opposite side of the gorge where the cliffs were nothing but a black expanse, pitch black. I could not see the river way below. All was quiet except for a faint rumble of gushing waters. A thin line of dim light lay along the far western horizon, delicate and wistful beneath the constellations.

But I needed to catch up with my aging pals. Nobody wants to be left behind. So I started along the path again, slowly, one clumsy step at a time, aided by the starlight from our bright galaxy.

• • •

You'll never believe what happened later that night after our Big Arsenic banquet. Per usual we had imbibed too much and Bubba passed out in my bed. Poor baby, he ached all over. Yuri and Sharon motored off to their motel room. That left me and the rich girl from Aspen, Marjorie Kittredge, alone at my kitchen table draining the final bottle of champagne. Marjorie was a slim young woman about thirty-five years old with brown hair cut short and pale gray-green eyes, no makeup. She wore a lavender Patagonia shirt and beige slacks and sandals, and seemed almost like a neutrally gendered tomboy, an odd choice for Bubba.

"Well, here we are," she said. "The last revelers standing."

We clinked jelly jars saying "Cheers" to each other, and swallowed the remaining drops of bubbly. Marjorie said, "Ah," and then, "What's next?"

I guessed that we should clean up the mess left by our celebration. She did not wish to deal with that aggravation. "Let's go out to our car instead."

I balked. "But you're Bubba's girl."

"Oh, don't mind him. He doesn't care. I just came along for the ride. We're not involved or anything."

I don't recall the make of Bubba's SUV; it was an oversized paean to conspicuous consumption. On a backseat bigger than a twin bed lay three pillows and a puffy, bright-red North Face sleeping bag. Marjorie explained, "I always bring along this stuff on a trip. If I'm carsick I take a Dramamine and survive by going to sleep."

Wrapped in the bag and comfortably cushioned, I held her while she talked. She gave off a healthy fragrance of being washed clean with mild soap. "I'm not very ambitious," she stated, "but I have a lot of money in a trust fund and other places. We grew up lavishly. I have three siblings; we aren't very close. My father invented a diagnostic machine that can predict some cancers before they appear. I'm not totally up on the gory details. I never even attended college. I was bright in high school, though; one year I skipped a grade. I consider myself a free spirit but most people say I'm irresponsible. I can't argue with that. I am not a prankster, I've never been jailed, I don't like to embarrass people by acting wild. I'm a terrific skier and also an organic vegetarian. I'm sorry if that shocks you. I guess it's sort of a downside to my personality. At least I can pay the hefty markups at Whole Foods. I went to meetings for a while until they bored me. Everybody was too fussy. I'm not a great fan of finicky people. And I could do without bedlam. I want everyone to be amenable. There are so many *agendas* out there. I try to maintain my composure at all costs. It's not apathy, but I like being relaxed, you know? Mostly, I avoid all the hubbub and do as I please, I'm lucky that way. I can fly all around the world whenever and wherever I want. You know, to Maui, Leh in Ladakh, Paris, whatever. I have a son who lives with his dad in London. We get along great and I love him dearly, but I'm not a very good caretaker. I don't really attach to many people. I'm leery of entanglements. I'm a wanderer, always curious about what lies around the next corner, yet I don't hang tough in one place or with one person for long. I have a short attention span. ADHD, you know. I like Bubba because he's fun to be with. He makes me laugh and he picks up the hotel and restaurant tabs. Most of my so-called friends never do that because I'm so rich they expect me to pay for everything. Oops, what's this? I'll be darned."

I apologized to her for having an erection. She asked,

"Do you want me to give you a blow job?" I said, "No, no, I'm sorry, it's nothing personal, it just happened."

Marjorie rustled under the sleeping bag, and, kneeling on the floor of the spacious car, she unzipped my fly and took me gently into her mouth. I had a shockingly terrific orgasm immediately.

"Do you feel better?" she asked, snuggling against me again with her head on my shoulder. "That seemed pretty energetic."

Then she continued with her soliloquy, unfazed by the brief interruption. "When I have sex with people I never experience orgasms myself. I have an ambivalent sexuality. I'm not a stickler for romance. I never flirt. You can't accuse me of being a coquette. But I like to talk a lot, talking is my orgasms. Words are very reassuring to me and I'm gratified when people don't squelch my verbose enthusiasms. It's the price people have to pay when they fuck me. I'll accept anyone as my confidant if they will only please be patient and listen. I'm infatuated with words, how they sound off my tongue. Ever since I was a little girl I loved to read dictionaries, isn't that odd? Is it too weird? I'm in love with *vocabulary*. Do you mind?"

"No. Not at all. Me too."

She yawned, and then her right hand probed around under the sleeping bag until she had grasped my limp penis, holding it in a friendly manner. "I've never been married," she continued. "I've had a lot of offers but I think most of them have been financially motivated. When you're this rich it's hard to trust peoples' hidden motives. I like you, you're not a bad fellow. Tell me when you want me to quit talking, I'm a serial talker. It's soothing to me. I can go on forever if you let me. I hope you don't think I'm trivial or just an aimless millionaire. You should know that I love being alive. My life is strangely happy."

I said, "It's okay. Talk all you want. I don't mind."

But then very shortly, all tuckered out, Marjorie fell asleep and I held her, under the sleeping bag, for hours, drowsing myself with her lips just barely pressed against my throat.

Six

On September 22, 1997, Yuri dropped dead of a heart attack on his New York City fire escape. Fifty-seven years old. It was the fifteenth year of our first Annual Big Arsenic Fishing Contest back in 1983. This year's contest had been slated for October 6. "He was smoking his pipe and watering the geraniums," Sharon sobbed into the telephone. "I found him when I got back from work and pulled him inside and then I sat in a chair and stared at him. I know you're not supposed to touch the body but I couldn't leave him out there, it had started raining. He just lay quiet and didn't move. I understood I should call the cops, but then everybody would come and take him away from me and people would be talking and riding up and down in the elevator and being sympathetic and asking me to fill in these forms and I couldn't bear the thought of all that commotion. I told Yuri to wake up but he didn't listen to me. Where did he go? He was talking to me this morning. We had a little argument because I keep telling him he smokes his pipe too much. He never listens. We loved each other. I should have been a stronger person about the pipe. I never understood how—"

"Stop, Sharon," I said. "It's not your fault. I promise. It's really really not your fault."

"It's *all* my fault," she said, totally bewildered. "Somebody else would have made him quit smoking. I wasn't adamant enough. I should have forced him to go to the doctor. He hated doctors. When he had pains in his chest he brushed them off cavalierly. But I should have insisted that—"

I said, "Please. These are all moot points. You did your best. He was a difficult human being born with a flaw in his heart before he ever met you. I'm sorry. I don't know what to say. The last time we spoke on the phone he gave me a lecture on Trotsky and the Fourth International. We laughed. He seemed fine. You can't ever tell. He was excited about coming out west in two weeks."

"This was not supposed to happen," she moaned. "He's only fifty-seven. It could have been avoided—"

She went on keening like that for too long. After the first five minutes I mostly listened to her express guilt over causing Yuri's death. When there was a pause, I said again, "It's not your fault, Sharon. I love you." Then she began excoriating herself once more, so bereft she did not know what she was saying. With another woman Yuri would have published his novels. With another woman he would have been happy. With another woman he would have had a better sex life. With another woman—

"With another woman he would have dropped dead twenty years ago," I interrupted. "You supported Yuri all your time together, Sharon. Nobody can impugn your devotion. You killed yourself going downtown to that family law practice every day to earn a living so that Yuri could work on his novels and travel on fishing assignments all over the globe and read his way through the entire canon of Western philosophy. He owed you everything. You have been an angel to him."

There followed a pause, a terrible silence. I could not hear anything on the other end of the line. Talk about eerie. It did not even seem that she was breathing. She emitted no sounds, no sobs, no sniffles, no nothing. Finally, I asked, "Sharon, are you there?"

She wailed, *"I'm here but I'm all alone!"* and hung up on me.

When I called back to check on her five minutes later she had figured out that Yuri died because she gave him the wrong vitamins and too much meat in his diet, and because she had never threatened to divorce him unless he quit smoking his pipe.

"I murdered him by letting him get away with that," she moaned.

What do you say to a woman who just lost her partner for life who also happened to be your dearest friend? A woman who is so overcome by the shock of her grief that she cannot possibly think straight? I can't believe what I said. I mean, I was as flustered and confused and dismayed as Sharon, so I thought I could somehow lighten our hearts with a joke. That's what tragedy does to you. I blurted, "Sharon, gird yourself. I'm going to call the New York City district attorney's office and order them to send a SWAT team to your loft to arrest you for dispatching your husband and they'll incarcerate you for the rest of your born days. If you have a cyanide capsule I'd take it now and save yourself a lot of trouble."

And then you know what transpired?

We both broke out laughing hysterically despite, or because of, all our anguish.

· · ·

I flew back to New York for the memorial service and Bubba also came on a redeye flight from Hollywood. *The Obnoxious Noseguard* had run into postproduction snags engendered by cost overruns, studio apprehensions, and the sudden expiration, from a cocaine/PCP overdose, of the film's director. Sharon embraced me, her face swollen from mourning. "What am I going to do?" she asked. "I loved him more than anything. He was my consolation. But I could never console him. And I never—"

"Please don't start, Sharon. I understand. I know. And I'm so sorry."

"I can't help it," she said. "I can't believe he's gone. I don't know how to think right now. I wasn't prepared."

"I can't think either," I said. Then I did not know what more to say, so I held her for longer than usual. Bubba stayed back a few feet, looking at the floor and at his fingertips and out the window and again at his fingertips, embarrassed by Sharon's dismay. I was embarrassed by it too because I had difficulty not crying myself. And then I let myself have at it, because what the hell? Bottom line, life's too short. If you need to grieve you should embrace the sorrow; you can't hold everything in forever even in a room full of strangers.

"I love you, Sharon," I said. "Yuri loved you too. He told

me a million times. You could take it to the bank and earn interest on it."

We squeezed each other hard. Then I disentangled myself and Bubba gave her a hug. He never took off his cowboy hat, so I had to remove it for him. Bubba was not an apostle of politesse. He grabbed back the hat and settled it upon his shiny golden locks that apparently had just been feathered by a Beverly Hills tonsorial crackpot. You have money, you spend it.

Sharon had set up two card tables with a white linen cloth spread over them, and on the cloth was arranged a montage of Yuri photographs. One picture was of a tough little kid from Strawberry Mansion standing beside a public trash can with a basketball lodged under one arm and a Pepsi in his other fist, grinning at the camera when he was only a gap-toothed eight-year-old. Also on the card table were photographs of Yuri on the job for his hook and bullet magazines, catching smallmouth bass in Arkansas, landing cobia off the Outer Banks, fly-fishing for bonefish in the Bahamas. Too, Sharon had included some of our Big Arsenic trailhead portraits, featuring me, Bubba, and Yuri flaunting our rod-case erections with the usual obstreperous gusto.

Forty people crowded Sharon and Yuri's loft near Canal Street where the eulogies were given. Friends and family from Philadelphia and New York. His father had died years ago but his mother came, a tiny stooped-over lady in her early eighties with gray hair and rimless glasses, who kept sidling over to an open window to take a few puffs from a cigarette. I had met her on a couple of occasions in Philadelphia after she retired from stitching garments for the mass-market chains. She was a tough old broad, name of Barbara, and she did not cry.

"I will miss my son," she admitted. "He was a difficult kid. Recalcitrant. He argued about everything. Eight years old, he wrote to the manufacturer of Shredded Wheat if a Straight Arrow cardboard was missing from the box. Ten years old, he accused me of being a hypocrite with my sister, Nadine, his aunt, who put on fancy airs and was not a communist. Twelve years old, he read the *Daily Worker*, front to back, after Phil was through with it. His father. Half the time he was late for supper I had to go fetch him from the basketball courts on the playground or from the pool hall. Jimmy's Pool Hall. All that energy in such a little body. When he was born he weighed eight pounds, thirteen ounces, he was a huge baby. You're looking at me? You're right, the delivery almost killed me. Then what happened? He stopped growing when he was five. That didn't matter. You see, I know I'm his mother yet I think that even a stranger would have credited him with stature."

"He had stature in my book," I said.

• • •

I forget if it was before or after all the palaver that a neighbor proficient with the bagpipes stood on a fourth-floor roof across the alley wearing a kilt and a Tam O'Shanter and played "Amazing Grace." That was sad and it ruffled everyone's heartstrings.

"Yuri was right," I said at the start of my eulogy, "there's no point in taking care of your teeth."

Then I tottered on for a while. I had written my talk

136

in a notebook during the flight from Albuquerque to New York. I reminisced about all the fun we'd had up in the mountains hunting grouse, down in the Río Grande gorge catching trout, drinking bourbon around my kitchen table, arguing about James Joyce and Thomas Pynchon. I grew mawkish and embarrassed myself by toting up the books Yuri had written yet never published; however, he had kept *trying*. I mentioned his credo: *What's the point of creating anything less than a masterpiece?* I should have cut it short but I didn't, and Yuri would have been appalled. He would have scorned my "lachrymose reverence," understanding it as "supercilious commiseration."

Half a dozen orators spoke after me. One of them was Bubba, who stood up to affectionately dwell upon the fact that Yuri was the biggest little man he'd ever met. "He was like a miniature tornado, a magician with words, he had a brain as complex as the infinite universe described in 'The Aleph,' that famous Jorge Luis Borges short story that Yuri admired. And I admire it also. Yuri knew something about everything, a walking encyclopedia, and he had been every-where . . ."

After the last homage people milled around ardently reminiscing about Yuri while snacking on a wide range of tasty canapés provided by Sharon and Yuri's friends. I was conversing again with Yuri's mom, Barbara, when, glancing over her shoulder, I noticed that Bubba loitered alone at Yuri's bookcase perusing the many titles. Just as my eyes settled on him, Bubba unzipped his briefcase and surreptitiously plucked a volume off the shelf, slipping it into the posh leather bag. Then he continued scanning the tomes as if nothing had happened.

Barbara said to me, "Yuri and Phil always shouted at each other. His dad. They gave me a headache. They argued at the dinner table. Even when he was four years old, Yuri shouted at his father. He really had a temper when things were unfair. I guess he would have lived longer if he'd known how to relax."

· · ·

Eventually, Bubba and I left Sharon to all the family members and we walked a few blocks north to a SoHo sidewalk restaurant on West Broadway between Prince and Spring Streets where the waiters dressed in black. We ordered osso buco and a bottle of expensive red wine compliments of my generous buddy. "I like your hat," our waiter said to Bubba. "Where are you from out west?"

"I'm from Lubbock, Texas," Bubba said, "where cotton is king and the Red Raiders rule and you better not fuck with me because I've got a twelve-inch dick."

"I'd like to see that dick," the waiter said. He scribbled on his order pad and tore off the sheaf, handing it to Bubba. "Here's my phone number if you're ever in the mood."

"Guns up," Bubba replied, pointing his index finger and raised thumb at the guy.

I said, "Bubba, what book of Yuri's did you steal at his funeral, you thief?"

Bubba looked at me wide-eyed, incredulous, gape-jawed, his eyebrows lifted, all innocence. "Huh? What are you talking about?"

"I saw you steal it. It's in your briefcase. Let me see that briefcase."

"There's nothing in my briefcase except personal business papers. Have you gone crazy? You should've stayed away from the Manischewitz."

"I saw you steal a book," I insisted. "Let me look inside your briefcase."

"No way," Bubba said. "Nobody but me looks inside my briefcase."

"Okay, here's the deal." I leaned forward. "If you don't show me the book you stole from our dead friend, I'm going to tip over this table into your lap and attack you. You know I'm nuts enough to do it. Then the waiters will jump on us, management will call the cops, and, in the melee, one way or another, I'm going to learn what book you stole from Sharon and Yuri. Fair enough?"

Bubba said, "I stole my own book back. Yuri never offered a nice word about it. Screw him and screw you. First he ignored it for years, and then when he finally read it he shit on it, and he also dumped on you for blurbing it, in case you don't remember. 'How much did I pay you for comparing it to *The Southpaw* and *North Dallas Forty*?' He sneered in contempt. It's a decent novel, and Yuri was an imposter who couldn't write his own way out of a paper bag. A literary snob. I flew all the way to New York to retrieve my book from that hard-ass. It's too good for his library. I despise Tolstoy *and* Proust."

"Show me the book," I said.

Bubba opened his briefcase and handed over a hard-cover copy of *The Obnoxious Noseguard*. He had dedicated it:

To Yuri and Sharon, my dear friends,
I hope you get some laughs out of this
little book I wrote. I love you guys.
                    Bubba

"You shouldn't have stolen it," I said.

"Sharon will never notice. She doesn't give a damn. As far as Yuri was concerned it was stinking up his book-case. So I removed the stink. He said it was 'a cliché from start to finish.' You heard him. He said, and I quote: 'It's so derivative, sophomoric, and jejune' that it embarrassed him. *'Jejune?'* What kind of a word is that? What does it mean? I'm not stupid, I looked it up. It took me a month just to figure out how to spell it. A librarian I knew scoped it out for me. Do you even know what it means you sniveling prep-school butthead?"

"I forget," I said. "I never used that word in one of my books."

"It means 'dull,' 'puerile,' 'insipid.' That's what he thought of my book. He called it 'a piece of toxic teenybopper bubble-gum,' remember? He said I didn't have an original thought in my head. He said when he took a shit 'the turds were shaped like the state of Texas.'"

"Yuri had a mouth. But so do you, so do I. Who cares? That's just our style and it's not the issue here. We loved Yuri. He was my best friend."

"*I'm* your best friend," Bubba said. "You lousy turncoat. You traitor. You pathetic codfish aristocrat."

I countered, "For a wealthy dullard you certainly seem to have a very specialized memory. And here I thought you never paid attention to a single thing Yuri said because you were always so absorbed in yourself that anything anybody else ever uttered was just white noise to you. But looky here. What a surprise. Sticks and stones may break your bones and names *can* actually hurt you. I'll be damned. Deep inside your antediluvian persona there's a teeny-weeny little human being scrabbling to escape."

"Very funny," Bubba said. "You think you're so clever. Yuri thought he was a big shot because he could crap all over me by blabbing about Jorge Luis Borges or some Dutch astronomer with a fake nose who fed leftovers to a mentally retarded dwarf he kept on a leash underneath his banquet table? What's that supposed to prove? Yuri had no clue how to survive in the *real* world. He was conceited and helpless. My soon-to-be-ex-wife Tawanda could eat Yuri for an appetizer before breakfast and pick her teeth clean afterward with his little bones."

My Texas buddy had grown too nefariously eloquent criticizing our mutual pal. So I said, "Okay, Bubba, that's enough. You're starting to piss me off. You are a very small man; in fact you are the dwarf on a leash. Correction, you're even smaller than a dwarf, you're a midget. Mental as well as physical. You want to know the truth? Yuri loved your book. Yet he was jealous. And angry at the world. And Yuri believed what Hemingway once said, that praise to a writer's face by his friends is the highest insult, fawning at its worst. Yuri never complimented me on any of my books and I never took it personal. And for the record, you've never complimented me on any of my books either you contentious envious twit."

"Give me back that book." Bubba reached for it.

I held it away from him. "Not until hell freezes over, Bubba."

He picked up his wine glass and said, "I'm going to throw this at you if you don't return my book in the next three seconds."

"It's not your book, it's Yuri's book."

"Yuri is dead, rest in peace."

"Then it's Sharon's book."

"She and her snotty husband hated my book together. Now I'm going to count to three," Bubba warned, "and then you are going to wish you never laid eyes on me in your life."

I could tell that the game was over and if we actually indulged in a physical altercation I'd likely go from atrial fib to ventricular death throes toot sweet. So I flipped him the book. He caught it expertly and shoved it into his briefcase, yanking shut the zipper.

"You're the biggest wuss I ever met," he said. And there was something in his face, in his flustered eyes, something poignant and foreign and so unlike Bubba it truly caught me by surprise. He was *aching*. And myself? I was totally fagged out, tired of all the bantering. Bubba and I needed to detach from the prison that long had held us. I felt terrible about Yuri. Let's staunch the bleeding, bag all this nonsense, and *grieve*.

Bubba said, "I don't care if his father had a number on his arm. What's it to me if he wasted his life repairing cheap watches instead of playing the violin?"

"Yuri was lying," I told him. "There was no number tattooed on his father's wrist, no violin. He just wanted you, for once, to acknowledge the sanctity of muteness."

"The *what*?"

Three teenagers walking abreast came strutting along the West Broadway sidewalk, one of them bouncing a basketball. They had on Michael jerseys down to their knees, baggy jeans with rolled-up cuffs, and high-top unlaced Air Jordans. As they passed our table one of the mini-goons grabbed Bubba's Stetson off his head and all three kids lit out like Jesse Owens at the 1936 Berlin Olympics. But they were messing with the wrong dude. Bubba kicked his chair over backward jumping to his feet and charged after them like a jacked-up linebacker shooting through the gap on a blitz. I had no idea he could be that fast, rotten knees and all and with a gut hanging over his belt.

Give the devil his due, Bubba still had reflexes, he was *explosive*. This would be the only glimpse I ever had of how he must have crashed into the opponents' backfields for Jason Rafferty at Texas Tech, and it was impressive. Who knows if Bubba had ever run a 4.5 forty in college, but I guarantee he ran one down the sidewalk now. Those little gangbangers had ten yards on him at the start, yet Bubba wanted his hat back and caught up to them as if he was wearing a nuclear-fueled jetpack and had a red-and-blue cape tied around his neck.

They were street-smart ruffians, however; you could tell

they had fled for their lives more than once from Italians or bloodthirsty Irish hoodlums chasing after them waving broken beer bottles or baseball bats. So when they hit the Spring Street corner, instead of continuing straight south they abruptly veered left at right angles eastward across West Broadway like characters in a Road Runner cartoon.

Even all these years after his competitive football days you couldn't fool Bubba, though. He still retained the traits that had made him a Red Raider standout. And at the Spring Street corner he cut left on a dime to cross West Broadway so close to the kids he could reach out and grab them. In fact, Bubba swung his right arm in a lightning fast swoop and his stubby fingers latched onto the rear brim of that white Stetson, plucking it adeptly off the kid's head. Then he staggered to a halt as the boys disappeared; they literally evaporated.

When he returned to our table, my friend sat down with a grunt, readjusted the hat on his head, snatched up the dessert menu, and while perusing it he informed me, "That's the *real* world out there, you chump, and Yuri never had a Chinaman's chance of publishing a book in it, let alone of earning more than sixteen grand a year writing his quaint ditties about peacock bass for the hook and bullet tabloids that paid him peanuts. Whattayou want for dessert? I'm having the crème brûlée."

Then Bubba abruptly dropped the menu and bowed his head, clapping both hands over his face as he cut loose a sob.

"Jesus Christ," he moaned, "Yuri's *gone*. Why are we fighting? I loved him. He was such an obstinate motherfucker.

He was so long-winded and superior. He was like a brother to us. I would have died for him. I wish I *had* died in his place. He was such an arrogant little prick. I've read that fucking 'Aleph' story twenty times since he pulled it on me down in the gorge and I *still* don't know what it means. He can *never* be replaced."

"So give Sharon back your novel," I urged, feeling my tear ducts about to be breached.

Bubba shook his head. "That wouldn't be right," he whimpered miserably. "Nobody calls my book 'jejune' and gets away with it."

Whereupon we suddenly let go of all pretenses, embraced each other, and—would you believe it?—we bawled.

• • •

The following day I flew back home and Bubba returned to Colorado. Due to some business crises over licensing fees and kickbacks at the Nevada brothels, he did not drive south to my hometown that autumn. So Bubba forfeited the first Big Arsenic fishing contest he'd missed in fourteen years. I spent the hours when we should have been boisterous on the Río Grande typing up another draft of a novel I'd been working on for a couple of years but never would sell. I had a character in my story who resembled Yuri, and another who could have been Priscilla Endicott—remember her? In my novel there is a third character who was their child that my imagination's Priscilla had given up for adoption at birth. You see, my fictional Priscilla had refused to have an abortion. Sometimes the child was a girl, Elena; at other times a boy named Casey.

Mostly it was the girl, Elena. I could envision her better. For the first two-thirds of my tale Elena was invisible, out of sight, not even part of the plot line until my Yuri character was dying of a brain tumor. Then I thought the child might suddenly appear to Yuri on a quest like that taken by many adopted kids to discover their birth parents. Yet I could not work out scenes of Elena's arrival at Yuri's bedside that did not seem melodramatic, sappy, carelessly invented. Yuri would not have approved. Many are the nights that I scanned through Charles Dickens's genius creations searching for ways to approach and hopefully solve my problem. So far I had not come across an answer. The narrator of my novel, a dead ringer for my actual self, did have a fantasy that one day, in his "real life," a letter to him would arrive out of the blue from Yuri and Priscilla's child asking him to tell her about her dad. By then, I suspect, Priscilla would have died from ovarian cancer. *Your dad was a rough, tough little cream puff,* my narrator began. *He taught me how to strut.* That letter never came. The real Yuri would have thought it grotesquely coincidental, pop art at its manipulative worst. Hence, my novel was sabotaged by self-destructive integrity. Even though it was Yuri I wished to honor, he must've been looking over my shoulder in disgust.

Although I had been a professional writer for thirty-four years, solving the dilemmas of novels never grew easier. I had published fourteen books of fiction and nonfiction and I'd been paid decent money to write twelve screenplays. Yet each project I worked on seemed more difficult than flying to Mars in a rocket ship and building a viable city on its surface of scorched rubble. Yuri's denigrating fusillades against my pandering work aside, it is not easy writing run-of-the-mill novels and being a dilettante.

Next year Bubba showed up behind the wheel of a monster white SUV with a scrappy bombshell named Nanci Farquar on his arm who was all flash and not an ounce of filigree, and we raced to the Río Grande like homesteaders in an Oklahoma land rush. Business as usual on the river, except there were only two of us now, and that felt weird. All-Bubba-all-the-time was not my idea of a mellow stroll through a summer meadow. That orotund imposter yelled at and bullied me with the usual affection, and I browbeat him in return with the same deprecating tenderness. You still had to come out fighting with Bubba or he would trample you flat as a piece of plywood. I suppose he thought the same thing about me.

However, the repartee was too raw, or it was too childish, I didn't like it. We had outgrown the clown act. I wished our contest was over, but we couldn't stop. Why is that? You get locked into the affliction (the *addiction*) and cannot escape. I tied the complicated blood knots on his leaders, and I dealt him the proper flies whenever he demanded them, and I carried extra equipment in my knapsack in case he smashed his reel or broke a rod tip or whatever. I also toted a first-aid kit with a tourniquet in it and some Percodan pills left over from my open-heart surgery. They say painkillers last forever.

I captured the 1998 title by a comfortable margin even though I could scarcely blunder through, around, and over the boulders anymore and had to set myself rigidly before casting so that I wouldn't do a face-plant into the river. And I won again in 1999 by a hair and a prayer. I noticed that Bubba was more adept on the river and I was totally slowing down. Age, the relentless equalizer. Though my heart problems were held at bay by various medicines, the oscillopsia truly cut my maneuverability. I had come to feel like the main character in a Three Stooges movie specializing in pratfalls. When I moved, the landscape before me and everything in it jounced and bobbled as if viewed through a handheld movie camera. Sad to say, yours truly did not have a fastball on the Río Grande anymore, I had to rely on fork balls and changeups and on a zany knuckler that bounced all over, so to speak. Junk. Smoke and mirrors. That's when you know the bell is tolling.

Sharon Adair called me up feeling lost two years after Yuri's death. She was still working downtown with the law firm and had grown as lonely as an old cat. "I can't find any little men with preposterous egos," she said. "They're all too tall and lacking in chauvinist qualities. They're so mincing and polite they make me grimace. Nobody would dare pinch my butt. I *hate* male feminists."

She kept Yuri's ashes in a box on the radiator by the window with the pipe he had been smoking when he died set atop the box. "One day I'll come out west and we'll throw his ashes into the Río Grande," she said. "Up at the Big Arsenic Springs."

"I'll be ready," I assured her.

• • •

Then the century turned and we survived Y2K, and Bubba

and I met again to promulgate the Annual Big Arsenic Fishing Contest, our eighteenth year, a remarkable run. This was on September 25, 2000, three years and three days after Yuri had died. *Tempus fugit.* I was still the one and only champ since our contest's inception, although I honestly wanted my domination to end. "Honestly?" Maybe that's embellishing a bit but you know what I mean. We were trapped in our personal *Groundhog Day* and I wanted out of the ritual. Yet how to escape? Since I couldn't seem to devise an exit strategy, the melody lingered on.

Bubba had stormed into my grubby domicile the night before shouting as loud as ever, his old grating self down to the molten core. *Plus ça change*, say the frogs, *plus c'est la même chose.* On the day of our contest Bubba berated me when I hooked the big ones and he tossed a couple of rocks. I lost my balance and fell into the river twice yet only sprained my pinkie. Occasionally, when we passed behind each other headed for the next pool, one of us said, "I really miss Yuri today," and the other answered, "Get out of my way, you palooka, I'm a very busy man." That was another expression Yuri had coined on the Río Grande.

I blew Bubba out of the water in 2000, same old, same old. He never had a chance. Blindfolded, locked in arrhythmia, gasping from asthma among the boulders, I could still rise to the occasion and crush him. Me and Stephen Hawking (and my oscillopsia be damned!). Bye-bye, Bubba. Off to a black hole with you. Taking countless tumbles, I bashed my shins, almost broke a kneecap, ruined one reel, bruised the heel of my right hand, and ripped out the butt seam of my filthy chinos. When we had the Official

Unveiling in my kitchen, witnessed breathlessly by Bubba's new Big Arsenic babe, Maggie Benoit, and by my old girlfriend and twice ex-wife, Rachel Ivory, Bubba produced only three modest trout specimens, which I countered tit for tat.

Did I say "Rachel Ivory?" Perhaps that is no surprise. As plain as day we were wedded to each other by an emotional golem reason could not explain. I was besotted by the terror of loving her, by the chaos and exaltation of our twisted ardor that needed to be reignited every handful of years. Beyond our mutual physical attraction resided a deep, and obviously irresistible, affinity that we held for each other's screwball magnetism; it kept goading us onto the battlefield strewn with corpses from our previous engagements. Excuse the excessive verbiage, but you should understand both of us were fascinated by the amorous butchery.

Even though Rachel was far and away the most level-headed and compassionate transformational therapist practicing in our town, and even though I, repeatedly, had been lauded for my literary accomplishments as if I were a grown-up and masterful explainer of life's confusing and often tragic concatenations, behind closed doors we were like a couple of suicide bombers running pell-mell toward each other. If you haven't been there, don't knock it, you don't know what you're missing.

My older daughter, Stephanie, said, "Dad, you're like a moth that keeps flying into the candle flame." Stephanie had three children now, Callie, Sally, and Roger. Her husband was a flight attendant for Southwest Airlines. My younger daughter, Naomi, said, "Pop, you're like a prize 4H cow that just wants to become hamburgers." Last year she had married her longtime boyfriend, a theoretical physicist at Los Alamos working on cold fusion for hydrogen-fueled power plants. And she had one year left at nursing school.

After Bubba's three trout specimens, I pulled from my droopy burlap bag a sixteen-inch rainbow and a seventeen incher, too. However, I wasn't done—drumrolls, *por favor*. My final fish tipped the scales at three pounds and twenty inches, a fat brown trout gleaming golden along his lower flanks, and that should have punched Bubba's button.

No reaction. Flat affect. He did not do a thing. Deadpan, he said, "Okay, you win, so what? This fishing contest is meaningless."

Right.

Then, still disconcertingly expressionless, he said, "You know something, you smug bastard? You pretend to be a good-hearted, compassionate Goody-Two-shoes, but underneath you're cruel. I don't think I like you."

Of course we laughed. Ha ha. I was a bit taken aback, though, as he poured us another round of champagne. Maggie Benoit wore a filmy piece of chiffon molded to her figure like damp silk, and when she gave me a snug embrace and kissed me she said, "You're cute. I like your style. But you're not for me. Frankly, I think you're too full of yourself and you shouldn't be. Where I come from a fish is just a fish, and fish are a dime a dozen."

Tilting her head she gave me a radiant smile, pressed her bosom and groin tightly against me with shocking boldness, then backed away, her eyes twinkling mischievously, happy to see my flustered reaction as she dissolved into Bubba's arms.

Rachel had no desire to fawn over me in public as if I'd just won the Indy 500. That had never been her bag. She liked Maggie Benoit and got a kick out of my embarrassment that Maggie had caused. I learned afterward that Bubba's girl had once been a bunny at the Dallas Playboy Club, and these days was happily married to a former professional basketball player (a point guard for the Mavericks) with whom she had three grown children. Currently, she was an assistant director of publicity and morality for the Dallas Cowboys cheerleaders. Where Bubba stood in her picture and in her estimation was a puzzlement.

We all drank oodles of champagne and recounted lighthearted jocular tales from when Yuri had been alive. Toward midnight, when Bubba and Maggie Benoit departed my house, that kleptomaniac absconded with the gaily painted wooden fish from Puerto Vallarta, our trophy all these years. I did not even register the theft because I was drunk . . . and later I could not produce an erection for Rachel.

Brushing off my apologies, Rachel gave me a comforting hug. "What are you worried about, darlin'? Take a Viagra."

"I *took* a Viagra," I said.

Rachel whispered into my ear, "I love you." She wrapped her arms around my torso, holding me in a reassuring way, which may have been the first occasion in our tarnished story of attachments and detachments that her clinch did not feel erotically stimulating but rather protective. And through my champagne fog I took note, waking up.

"I love you back," I replied, on tenterhooks. Yet I hastily added, "Please don't take it the wrong way."

"Don't panic," she said. "I'm not afraid of you anymore."

"'Afraid' of me?" I pretended to be shocked.

"I'm terrified of anyone who kidnaps the irrational part of me that sabotages my need to be myself," she explained, smiling. "You know that. It's my marital tradition."

Something happened. I'm not saying a flying saucer swooped down and hovered above the headboard, its open cargo doors illuminating us with beatific light. Yet maybe this night was the first time I'd halfway "honestly" fallen in love with Rachel. Cliché alert! You can be obsessed with somebody but never actually treat them like a human being. And a lover held on too high a pedestal is a calamity waiting to happen. That said, from here on it would be a new ball game between Rachel and yours truly and difficult for us to push each other away as we had before. A Eureka moment had occurred, developing casually, out of frame, in secret, unbeknownst to us. When our tectonic plates shifted a few inches the world changed. Although we barely felt the shiver of realignment, it would be lasting. This is an unconscious acclimation, a bit of physical and emotional magic that nobody quite understands and for which everyone yearns.

Subsequently, Rachel and I continued to avoid sharing a dwelling because that would have been stretching the point. Instead, we carried on our separate lives, meeting once a week to break bread, see a movie, hike in the high mountains, or to indulge ourselves between the sheets. You could say we managed to strike a happy medium at last by avoiding (like the plague) the sort of familiarity that breeds contempt. Some folks might consider such an arrangement quirky, but hey:

To each his own, and the devil take the hindmost.

Seven

That obdurate scion of Lone Star born-agains blind-sided me the next year only seventeen days after Al-Qaeda flew their planes into the World Trade Center and the Pentagon. You'd think that I would have been ready for it but I was not, even though I wanted Bubba to win the damn contest and get it over with so I could relax, take five, and move on to my next reincarnation. It's true, I was so sick and tired of never having lost the Annual Big Arsenic that I wanted to run around in circles screaming and tearing my hair out. *Seriously*. After a while, even victory stinks. I know, because ever since my seventh birthday I have hated the New York Yankees.

Still, watch out what you wish for, you just might get it. I bet nobody would have been prepared for a tragic surprise ending the likes of which now transpired. So stay glued to your seats and don't switch the channel, this chapter is the payoff of my convoluted morality tale. Maybe Bubba finally rattled me with his bombast, I don't know. Or it could be I merely suffered a bad day, it happens to everyone sooner or later. Yuri and I had once seen Sandy Koufax shelled at Shea Stadium by the cellar-dwelling New York Mets, chased in the fourth inning during a year when he pitched a no-hitter for LA and garnered another Cy Young Award.

I would certainly never blame my lack of success to oscillopsia, atrial fibrillation, or my crippling disequilibrium. Please, give me more credit than that. Real Men don't make excuses, ever. Bubba showed up in Paradise for the first time without a lollapalooza on his arm, freaked because he had recently turned fifty and had an elevated PSA. "I'm having a run of bad luck," he explained. "It's the curse of Tawanda and this endless divorce from hell. I agreed to give her the US Mint but now her lawbooks is asking for Fort Knox, too. I can't believe we're still on the mat all these years later and I haven't pinned her yet. Pretty soon I'll have to hire a hit man, though they don't come cheap these days. I swear I'm gonna wind up whacking that broad and I won't mind doing the time."

Rachel had not attended the pre-contest ballyhoo tonight because 9/11 at the World Trade Center twin towers had killed one of her childhood friends and she was in no mood for Big Arsenic antics. "Why didn't you call it off?" she remonstrated. "Have you no feelings?"

My rejoinder? "You can't allow tragedy to stifle all the fun."

"But you do realize what our country's revenge will look like, don't you?"

"Yes. However, I can't think about that right now. I'm indulging my built-in genetic protective device for survival."

Rachel said, "When you get home tomorrow night don't call me. I'll let you know when I feel friendly again."

"Fair enough." I stifled an urge to apologize, recant, beg her to reconsider. We were "grown-ups" now.

Bubba and I sat in my diminutive kitchen drinking bourbon on the rocks with maraschino cherries, tying leaders and discussing all of tomorrow's possibilities, two aging Goliaths not even pretending to be young. I don't know why, given my health problems, I was slurping up the Wild Turkey. For whatever reason, recent terrorist events plus the Annual Big Arsenic had made me inanely macho. The rest of the year Rachel and I drank Perrier, vanilla soy milk, and Odwalla fruit smoothies.

"Tomorrow I am your Osama bin Laden," Bubba said. "Your worst nightmare. Tomorrow you finally eat the big one, buddy. You lose. The Saddle Tramps are gonna ring my victory bells. I pity you with all my heart."

"Where's my fishing trophy?" I demanded. "I won't compete unless you give it back to me."

"It's not 'your' trophy. I left it at home. I'm going to massacre you this year, so technically it already belongs to me."

I decided not to feed his manic childishness by arguing. And actually, I didn't care about the trophy, did I? After all, it was only a piece of wood and I was in a dither to pass it on, getting off the schneid. Bubba could keep the thing even if I knew in my heart that he would never legitimately win our contest. Why not? It's simple: I was unbeatable.

I would have to do a Dutch act for him to triumph. But I was ready to go for broke because I had finally realized that winning too often is a loser's game. It takes the fun out of everything. *Nobody* anymore roots for US Steel. And when was the last time you voted for a Kennedy?

"So what happened to *The Obnoxious Noseguard* movie?" I asked.

"The studio recut the entire film and only released it in Croatia."

(And, for the record—though not to be vindictive, mind you—it never even came out on video.)

· · ·

Our contest day was an oddball experience, hot yet overcast, not as menacing as it should have been given what would soon transpire. I was hungover from last night, feeling poorly, and my heart fluttered out of sync. Bubba appeared in a sour mood, too, his insults more rote than rollicking, just phoning them in like robot calls. Nevertheless, when we reached the rim of the gorge and gazed upon the silvery river far below all was forgiven because Paradise is always Paradise, it says so right in the Bible. And everybody wants to prolong an experience that once brought them bliss. We posed for a rod-case erection self-portrait and then kissed the Vanilla Tree, but when we reached our usual commencement spot on the shoreline above Little Arsenic Springs, Bubba suddenly realized that he had left his fishing vest up in the car. *What?* And I had never noticed.

"You're kidding," I said.

"Look at me, am I wearing my vest?"

"You're kidding," I said again. "I don't believe your incompetence."

"Shut up and hand over some of your flies. It's your

fault, you should have noticed. I have a million things on my mind. I actually work for a living. I'm a tycoon. All you do is write pablum for people suffering from arrested development. And give me a reel," he added. "My reel was in the vest."

I relinquished the flies and an extra reel from my knapsack, then I had to tie him two new leaders because the ones I'd fashioned last night also occupied his missing vest. This peeved me, given that I had very determined plans of going into the tank for him. Talk about irony.

The river was high and murky, I don't know why, not because of recent rains, believe me. Maybe from irrigation releases up north in Colorado filled with fertilizer and herbicides. I made our leaders short for this muddy water because the fish would not be able to see very far. "Fat black beadhead woolly boogers," I said, "on the tail fly *and* the dropper." What we should have done was dig a few worms and catch a couple of chubs, filet them, thread the filets onto size 4 snelled hooks, and drop them into the river weighted by Champion spark plugs.

Too bad that was against the rules.

I felt listless, not a good sign. I was wheezing uncomfortably. The dirtied Río Grande was going to be a challenge—so what? A pro can win (or throw the contest) under any conditions, and of course I'd give it my all. Anything less would be an insult to Bubba, right? Unfortunately, I could not tease up a bite at first, and neither could Bubba. Navigating the boulders with no balance whatsoever was, for me, a masochistic endeavor. I felt like a victim of multiple sclerosis, muscular dystrophy, and either a major stroke or a direct hit by lightning. It loomed as a bad day on the black rocks.

No complaints, however. God forbid.

Conditions change, and after a while the itty-bitty fish had a flurry of hunger, which enabled me to hook three seven-inch browns that I quickly threw back. Sardines! Bubba landed a couple of minnows also, then the river went dead again. So far no keepers. We continued fishing hard in our blustery style, which was not conducive to those conditions given the lack of back eddies and shallow riffles to plumb. The river was moving too fast, it was too deep and murky, hence after an hour and twenty minutes I realized that even a single qualifying trout could win the day.

At that point a psychopath atop the western rim of the gorge fired a rifle shot that echoed throughout the canyon, terrifying me. The adrenal boost knocked my heart for a loop as a bullet deflected off a rock forty yards south of us. A brace of explosions followed. The canyon amplified sound times ten, times twenty, the reports were *loud*; they made me jump and I scrambled behind a rock almost pissing in my pants while Bubba remained in the open, unafraid, arrogantly displaying his borderline IQ.

"What is the matter with you?" he asked. "Why are you crouched behind that rock?"

"Because I'm petrified!" I yelled.

"Relax, he's not shooting at us."

"How do you know that?"

"Look at me. Am I dead? Is there a hole in my head?"

"There's a *huge* hole in your head underneath that Stetson!"

Two more shots sounded that pierced me with their detonations. I heard a slug carom off somewhere not too distant with a scarifying whine. After Bubba had climbed onto a boulder to make himself a better target as he jiggled his woolly boogers in the froth and foam, he yelled over at me, "For every minute you don't fish while guns are going off, you lose a point!"

A subsequent report echoed as if fired inside a granite cathedral—*BAM!* And then *AM! AM! AM! AM! AM!* bouncing south between the walls.

Next, while I remained crouched for shelter behind my basalt shield, Bubba hooked a big cutbow—*oh no!* He became so excited he fell off his perch into knee-high water, but recovered and backed to shore holding the rod high, fumbling behind himself for his net as he shouted, "Give me a hand here, you coward! This is a good one. I need help!"

"Land your own fish!" I cried from behind my rock. "Those are the rules!"

Another blast caused me to squawk, I couldn't help myself. The bullet splattered against a megalith way downstream.

"If I lose this trout you're to blame," Bubba said, onto the shore by now in thick grasses where he threw down the useless rod and, I swear to God, began hauling in the line hand over fist.

A final *boom!* sounded. Imagine a big car backfiring six inches from your ear. The echo rattled along the canyon's length, banging back and forth off cliff walls, and I never heard a ricochet.

There is no justice on earth. Bubba did not lose that prize because G-d loves the meshuganas among us. He backtracked, hauling the fish in by jerks and yanks, and, with a last furious heave on the line, impelled it ashore, a truly ignoble landing worthy of the Keystone Kops. However, I've been there, done that, so I can't be throwing stones. Bubba grabbed the squirming trout and bashed it dead against a rock and held it up for my dismayed edification—a laudably chunky sixteen-inch cutbow. I knew at once that it spelled doom, yet I wanted him to wear the crown, *n'est-ce pas*?

"It's over," Bubba said. "I'm the champ, you're a has-been." He raised the cutbow toward the sky like Captain Ahab with a tiny white whale. "Hey, Yuri, look at this!" And then he told me, "You're dead. My ship has arrived."

"Not yet. The day isn't over," I reminded him.

Bubba extended the trout toward me. "Put it in your croker sack, okay?"

"Are you off your rocker? I'm not carrying your fish for you."

"Come on, come on," Bubba said impatiently. "I don't have a vest. And my pockets aren't big enough."

I did not believe his gall. "If I carry your trout it will get mixed up with my bigger fish, then you'll claim one of them was yours. I know you."

Bubba said, "You're not going to catch anything. Here, take it, hurry up, I wanna go back to work."

"No way. Have you no limit to how low you'll stoop to insult another person?"

"Okay. Fine. You refuse? Then I'm throwing this fish back in the river and I quit the Annual Big Arsenic Fishing

Contest. It's all over because you don't have the sportsman-ship or the compassion or the simple human decency to do me this favor when I'm at a disadvantage."

"Go ahead, Bubba, toss it."

"You asked for it. Here goes."

When Bubba pivoted sideways and reared to fling his cutbow into the Río Grande, I understood instantly the implications of this despicable act and all the argument that would follow, leading to emotional and intellectual confu-sion that would destroy eighteen wacky yet fun-filled years of our punch-drunk fishing contest. I was being black-mailed by a master at the craft, a morally comatose human being. He knew that I wanted to win more than I hated his scurrilous behavior. What he didn't know was that I was hoping to lose because I was sick of being unvanquished.

"*Wait!*" I cried. "*Give me the fish.*"

Bubba obliged, and I dropped it into my empty bag feel-ing dizzy and enraged.

"And don't forget to dampen it," Bubba ordered as he trotted off, craving to harvest more booty from the Río Grande. I stared after him doing the Valsalva maneuver, and this time it worked. My heart clicked back into sinus rhythm.

· · ·

Immediately, the day turned really miserable. I bit off my tail-fly woolly booger and tied on a spruce matuka, receiv-ing no action on the streamer, so I tried a muddler minnow instead. That fly generated no activity either, causing me to detest the river almost as much as I loathed my fishing companion. After all these years Bubba's personality and his tactics had finally gotten my goat. His weighty kill in my sack had become a jeering disparagement grafted against my hip. To make matters worse, I didn't think I could face his gloating. What if he really paid for a full-page ad in the *New York Times*?

Then I sucked it up and went back to work, employing every trick I could think of, yet I was not able to goad forth even one minnow's nibble. You look at a river, you know if it's dead or lively, and I knew that this river had now become as embalmed as a Sunday afternoon in Peoria. We were running out of light when Bubba passed me once more heading higher, all business, attacking the Río Grande as if he were still wearing pads and a helmet on the gridiron. And I could tell that he could smell it: *victory.*

Come dark I wouldn't quit and neither would Bubba as long as I showed the minutest bit of breath. He knew that a single fish landed by yours truly at the end could defeat him, hence if I did not leave that uncooperative river he would not depart either. We were both trapped in the Río Grande's abyss.

"It's over," he said. "It's too dark to fish."

Darkness is my enemy. When my eyes can't see clearly I have no balance at all. But I said, "Not for me, I still have plenty of light." Even then I aspired to hook a slippery titan I could throw back when he wasn't looking so that in the end his victory would be my "gift" to him. Go figure. The human species is warped. Given the dark of nightfall I could scarcely walk. I staggered like a hopeless drunk. At times, with my rod clamped by my teeth, I had to crawl on my hands and knees through the grasses and sand between boulders.

Bubba stripped line off his reel, casting into the darkness where he could only hear the roaring waters and see only the dolorous night.

Finally I gave up.

"Yes, it's over," I said with the deepest crestfallen sigh I had ever breathed in my life. "You win. I give up." Reeling in my line, I plopped down on a modest boulder staring dumbly at the bloody Río Grande. "That river stepped all over my blue suede shoes."

Bubba settled eight feet away displaying a wide Cheshire smile on his pissy visage.

"You didn't catch any fish?" he asked.

"Nope." There was no point in subterfuge. "Not that qualified as keepers."

He did not smell a rat. He knew I was telling the truth and mulled that over in his petite noggin for a thoughtful moment. Then he puffed up slightly. "So I'm the champ?"

"Yeah. You're the champ." Though I expected a huge sense of relief, it sure hurt to speak those vile words. Losing this combat to Bubba would be like getting depantsed by drunken fraternity boys in front of Marilyn Monroe. The stigma, the disgrace, the belittlement already had me so dejected I felt like jumping into the river and drowning myself.

Bubba removed his white Stetson and buffed the front of it with a few back-and-forth passes of his elbow, replaced the hat, and said, "Give me my fish. I want to look at it." He was really going to rub it in, the lout. Yuri would have called him a "demonic algolagnist." Don't ask me, I'm not in the mood; look it up.

I untied my burlap sack and tossed it at his feet. Bending down, he removed the sixteen-inch cutbow, a handsome fish, and admired it. I hated him as he turned it over a couple of times, the swaggering showboat. He kissed it on the snout.

Bubba said, "That's ten points for biggest fish and two points for most fish and one point for first fish. I beat you thirteen to nothing."

"That's right," I admitted glumly, bracing myself.

"I beat you thirteen to *nothing*," he repeated.

I couldn't argue with him. I was totally tapped out and thinking, *I'm too old for this malarkey.* I knew a barrage was coming and did not look forward to it. I understood that a man of Bubba's nature wouldn't lose the Annual Big Arsenic Fishing Contest eighteen years in a row as he had without building up an enormous backlog of frustration, resentment, and potential unsportsmanlike gleefulness when he finally managed to hoist the trophy. And I also accepted that I had it coming—my comeuppance. You live by the sword you die by the sword. I deserved whatever sordid punishment he dished out, I welcomed it, in fact, but it was going to be an ordeal and I was dreading the nightmare. Yet if I had any class at all I would bite the bullet and throttle my rancor, avoiding all self-pity.

"Let's get out of here," Bubba said. "It's dark and a long way up."

"Okay."

When he tried to hand over my damp bag I said, "Excuse me?"

The transparent charlatan acted taken aback. "What do you mean?"

"I'm not carrying your fish out of this canyon. You caught it, you lug it."

Bubba said, "Fine, fine, you don't have to get huffy."

He twisted the mouth of the sack and pulled it up underneath his belt at the hip and tucked under the excess burlap again and adjusted it a couple of times. Then he grinned at me.

"This feels *good*," he said.

I'll bet it did.

Bubba added, "Yuri never won this contest. He never even came close. Slothrop reigns supreme."

• • •

We remained quiet as we hobbled up the side of the canyon, zigzagging back and forth on the long steep switchback trail, both of us self-conscious, I guess, about the changing of the guard. I couldn't figure out his reticence. By now he should have been bombarding me with every boastful blasphemy in his arsenal of vengeful hyperbole. What was holding him back? Perhaps he could not yet fathom his miraculous good fortune. My triumphal streak ever since the contest's inception had blown everything out of proportion. Imagine if Green Bay had won the first eighteen Super Bowls how the winners of Super Bowl XIX might have felt—for Bubba it must have been something like that. Or like the Brooklyn Dodgers felt in 1955 after finally defeating those execrable Yankees: stunned, speechless, disbelieving.

I could really feel my sixty-one years. Sixty-one is *old*. Bubba was only fifty and he was pooped too. The enormity of his conquest had not truly sunk in yet. I didn't have a flashlight because the narrow beam doesn't provide a wide-enough landscape to give me visual balance. I walked wide-legged and slowly, repeatedly thumping my rod case down hard. Every fifty yards Bubba halted to let me catch up. He asked twice, "Are you okay?" I said, "Yeah, I'm fine. What's it to you?" His solicitous nature reeked of hypocrisy; I knew he was setting me up for a clobbering. Still, he remained subdued, refusing to mention the outcome of our day on the river. What was the matter with him? What sort of iniquities was he cooking up in his pea-sized noodle? Get it over with, already, Marquis de Bubba. I reviled him, the creep. He belonged in a George Romero movie—*Night of the Living Bubba.*

Up higher we paused, drinking deeply of the cool arsenic waters from our plastic bottles while overhead the Milky Way shone brightly peppered across the sky. We could hear the faint roar of turbulent waters far below, then a breeze came along; it was warm and we could smell a vanilla odor mixed with sage and dust. We surveyed our darkened kingdom, the faint glittering ribbon of river miles below, the black canyon walls, the starry sky, and nowhere an artificial light or another human being.

"I love this gorge," Bubba said.

"I love it, too," I said. What was *wrong* with me? Both of us reeked of false sincerity, phony piety, mendacity, two-faced mealymouthed perfidious sanctimony. What a bunch of hooey. And all the while I could *feel* his Enola Gay droning toward me.

· · ·

We made it to Bubba's car, fetched beers from the cooler, opened them up and swigged deeply while slumped at a nearby cabana's picnic table, absorbing the quiet ambience, gazing around, awed by the twinkling universe. I awaited the commencement of his mean-spirited deluge, yet still nothing transpired. Bubba said, "I wish Yuri was here. Why did he have to die?"

"I know. I miss him, too." I had become almost lulled by his mellifluous tones.

Bubba whispered, *"Shuttup, I know what I'm doin'."*

We laughed. We almost cried.

Then again Bubba said mournfully, "I wish he was here to savor this."

And I honestly confided, "Me, too. It's been a long time coming. I'm actually relieved. Yuri would have been proud of you. He would have enjoyed this occasion."

Then I clammed up because I could hear myself being pathetically—correction *bath*etically—obsequious, a servile, truckling bootlicker. The Racket Ranch pooh-bah had actually *defeated* me; I hadn't even been talented enough to take a dive. When you know justifiable retribution is coming down in droves upon your aching head it is morally repugnant to try and ingratiate yourself in order to mitigate the severity of the inundation. Even a fish wouldn't get caught if it kept its mouth shut.

Soon we were on the deserted Wild River access road slowly cruising north along the paved route winding through sagebrush and piñon trees, working on our second beers, Bubba behind the wheel of his rococo gas-guzzler. We watched for owls and coyotes and for little mice scampering across the road. A few minutes into our trip, Bubba began to speak.

"I apologize for all that garbage I spouted on the day we went to Yuri's memorial in New York," he said. "I didn't mean any of it. I was just upset that he was gone. Yuri had more soul in his little finger than both of us have put together in our entire bodies. He was his own man, and how many of us can say that? I've spent my entire life kissing asses or having my ass kissed by shrimps who are smaller than me. I walk around shaking my big shoulders to keep all my employees trembling in their boots. People aren't intimidated by weakness—you have to crack the whip. Most of them don't like me but I have the money so they keep their mouths shut, bow and scrape and jump out the window if I say 'jump.' Yuri is the only person I've ever known who wouldn't take crap from anyone. I *respected* him, and that's really rare for me. I live in a world where everybody wants to steal your wife, rob your house, embezzle from your bank account. All your so-called friends are enemies although it's 'nothing personal.' But Yuri was honest. When we were down on the river that time yelling at each other the last day we fished together I was scared to death it might wind up in a fight because he would've killed me. Yuri was the toughest human being I ever met. He had genuine rage and righteousness on his side. I don't care if he lied about his dad and the violin. Water over the dam. He refused to be a hypocrite even if refusing to be a hypocrite destroyed him. He had *principles*. The only person I know who can compare to him is my brother, Brian. When we were kids we wrestled a lot and even though he was way bigger than me I used to rub his face in dog shit on our lawn because when we wrestled Brian always followed the rules, he couldn't use an illegal hammerlock or kick me in the balls or bite my neck to make me let go of him. I had none of those restraints myself, so I could whip him handily. Sure, Yuri was a much different person from Brian, yet he also had those restraints. All the rest of us are just cheaters and liars. Every night that I go to bed after another day of browbeating humanity I feel ashamed of myself. I hate capitalism just as much as you do. When I die I'll go directly to hell. Maybe I'll meet Yuri down there but with him it'll be different. He can stand the heat. Who else do you know who you can say that about? I loved Yuri. I love you too though not in a limp-wristed way, of course. But I loved Yuri in a different way because he *was* different. He was *noble*. You and me, we're paddling upstream in the same canoe, we're just petty human riffraff, part of the thundering herd, a couple of jejune automatons. Our egos are so stupidly predictable. Yuri didn't have a paddle; he didn't even have a canoe. But he was *honorable*. I'm truly sorry I stole that book at his funeral. How could I be so small-minded? I was freaked out by his death. I am a very stunted and insignificant human being, just like you. It happened in a fit of pique."

When Bubba used the expression "in a fit of pique," alarm bells should have gone off, although by then I was almost as captivated by him as I'd been enchanted by Jimmy Stewart in *It's a Wonderful Life*. I'm surprised over-sized dewy globules chock-full of sodium weren't dribbling down my face.

Up ahead a small deer froze, caught by our headlights while standing in the middle of our path, and Bubba hit the brakes. It was a pretty doe hardly larger than a coyote, poised on her delicate tiptoes staring at us the same way we stared at her.

Bubba said, "Wow, look at that. Don't we have all the luck?"

"Yup," I replied warmly. "We have all the luck." I was feeling woozy after the beers and torn to pieces by Bubba's prattle, thinking it wasn't so bad after all to lose the Big Arsenic fishing contest. Maybe, at last, my funny friend, my wicked valentine, had decided to be mature. At last we had both undergone an important rite of passage. Bubba being magnanimous in victory was another interesting concept, yet the world is full of surprises. Maybe even yours truly could be magnanimous in defeat. Wouldn't *that* be a marvel.

Bubba put the shifting lever in park and opened his door.

"Where are you going?" I asked.

Without warning, he wigged out completely and started running in circles around the car, waving his cowboy hat and shouting, "I'M THE CHAMP! I'M THE CHAMP! I'M THE ANNUAL BIG ARSENIC CHAMP!" The frightened deer bounded away into the dark sagebrush as Bubba went crazy doing laps around the car at a full-tilt sprint.

"YOU LOSE! I BEAT YOU FAIR AND SQUARE! I'M THE CHAMP! I'M THE BIG ARSENIC CHAMP! WHO'S THE CHAMP? *I'M* THE CHAMP! I'M THE GREAT BIG BIG ARSENIC CHAMP!"

After six laps he jumped back into the SUV and spun the rear tires, lurching away so that we smelled burning rubber for the next quarter mile, and he floored the gas pedal so that we were instantly going seventy on this narrow winding piece of rural macadam in the middle of nowhere, which of course gave me an adrenal burst of terror throwing me right into a major atrial-fibrillation attack as I gasped, "Hey, slow down!"

"FUCK YOU! AND THE MAYFLOWER! AND THE DECLARATION OF INDEPENDENCE! I'M THE CHAMP!"

"Slow down!" I bleated. *"Please!"*

Fat chance of that. I closed my eyes. It was like a rocket launching at Cape Kennedy. I knew I was going to die and I almost did. He lost it. He hit a soft shoulder or something, I don't know what, but he skidded off the road into the sage-brush and churned and bounced and rocked helter-skelter from side to side with bushes slapping against our doors and against the undercarriage, and dust filled up the vehicle, and I experienced a vertigo spell that lasted until well after Bubba had miraculously steered us back onto the road almost tipping over in the process and had slowed down at last, still yelling repeatedly, "I'M THE BIG ARSENIC CHAMP!"

Then he said in his ordinary voice, "Open me another beer, I'm thirsty. Hurry up."

I was huddled against the door, dizzy and weeping now from fear, and then I started to vomit. Bubba braked, shouting, "NOT IN MY CAR!" and he reached past me, banging open the door, and pushed me out. I fell onto the ground barfing, and puked until I had almost ripped out my stomach lining with Bubba hovering over me saying, "Hey, are you okay? *You deserve this, you yellow-bellied, preppy East Coast, four-eyed Commie nerd, for all the years you humiliated me, you no-good rotten excuse for a human being . . .* but are you okay?"

"You bastard," I said. "Leave me here. I'll never ride in a car with you again. I've had it. You are insane." I was *pissed.*

When I had calmed down he helped me back to my seat. Bubba opened himself another beer and we proceeded east again through sagebrush and piñon toward the highway at a more normal rate of speed. He punched in a Dwight Yoakam CD and we listened to that for a mile. You can imagine that I was in cataclysmic shock. Every ten seconds Bubba would say, "Who's the champ?" And I would mumble, "You're the champ." I had no more pluck left in me, I just wanted to reach home alive and drink my Metamucil, pop an Ambien, and crawl into bed. I was sixty-one years old, for God's sake. Have pity on me.

"That's right," Bubba said, "I'm the champ. Who's the champ?"

"You're the champ," I said.

"Louder."

"You're the champ," I said, louder.

"That's right, I'm the champ. And you know what else?"

"No, what else?" I groaned.

"I'm the *champ*," Bubba said. And he spelled it out: "C-H-A-M-P!"

That did it. I opened the door and fell out again, rolling a couple of times as I bounced into the sagebrush and came to rest relatively unharmed except for some minor lacerations on my arms and cheeks from dead branches and little rocks. Horrified, Bubba braked and banged open his door and jumped onto the pavement all in the same motion after jamming the automatic transmission stick by mistake up into reverse instead of all the way up into park. And, as he sprinted around the back of the vehicle to come rescue me, the SUV surged to the rear on its own, knocking Bubba down and running right over him, then it continued south at ten miles an hour while Bubba shouted, "*Wait! Stop!*" He tried to bolt upright and give chase but suddenly pitched forward and died from a brain embolism just as the SUV veered to the right off the macadam, collided against a large rock at a peculiar angle, and tipped over. The headlights blinked out and the motor stalled.

Holy shit.

What had just *happened*?

I remained frozen, incredulous, for God knows how long. A few seconds? A few minutes? Then, feeling sick and terribly frightened, I crawled hastily through dry grasses, pebbles, and prickly pear cacti over to Bubba and stared at him. His eyes were wide open and there wasn't a mark on his face, or, as far as I could tell, a drop of blood on his beautiful head of luxuriously graying hair. I could hear his SUV gurgling in the background. Sometimes, despite being stupefied, you know immediately that somebody is dead even if their death makes absolutely no sense at all. I say that never having seen anyone else die abruptly in my life, but it must be instinctual.

Everything changes so *quickly.*

Bubba was very still. As frozen as stone. As motionless as if he'd been struck by a bullet to the heart. Beyond resuscitation. Artificial respiration would do no good. The world around us was abnormally quiet. I mean, except for the dripping auto liquids and crackles of the cooling engine, there were no other sounds, nobody to talk to, and we were surrounded by sagebrush and some piñon and juniper trees. No moon shone, yet all the bright stars of the Milky Way were afire and casting a silvery glint upon us.

Placing my hand on Bubba's neck, I felt the sting of a few cactus spines in my fingertips. They were not lodged deeply, and, despite the darkness, I pulled them out and laid my hand on him again. You're supposed to feel for a pulse. There was no pulse. You're supposed to straddle the body and press your hands—one atop the other—down on his chest at the sternum, pumping down and releasing, pumping down and releasing, restarting the heartbeat. So I did that. I straddled him and pressed down and let up about fifteen times, but nothing doing. It was so awkward and unbelievably strange. No air issued from his mouth. No sighs or whooshes or anything. I assumed I was applying pressure incorrectly but that didn't matter because it was hopeless anyway. Some coyotes gabbled shrilly from way over on the other side of the gorge. But only for a moment.

I got off of him and grew dizzy, suffering another vertigo attack, and, with my face pressed against the ground,

I grabbed hold of Bubba's arm to keep my spinning body from being ripped away and hurled off into the galaxies. My heart chugged and bumped erratically. The gravity of swirling space nearly yanked me into infinity. Me and Bubba together. I shrieked, "Stop it! *Please stop it!*" Then the vertigo ended. Breathless, I waited, spooked almost senseless. After a minute or two, warily, I lifted my head again. I felt sick to my stomach as my heart gradually relaxed. The entire experience was too freaky, it really scared me. I mean *really.*

"Bubba," I said, letting go of his arm. And maybe I was channeling Sharon with Yuri when I urged, "Hey, Bubba, come on, *talk* to me."

He didn't say a word. So I licked the tip of my finger and touched it to his shoulder making the "*Sssst!*" sound and drawing my hand away abruptly as if I had tapped a burning coal. He did not move a muscle nor blink his eyes nor give an obnoxious chuckle. How could he not respond to anything? How could this craziness be real?

"Hey, Bubba. Nobody gets a percentage of the gross. Can you hear me?"

Evidently not.

"Listen up, Bubba," I said. "Quit playing possum. Guns up, you asshole."

It was too late for all of that.

And it was my fault, too, wasn't it?

I was still channeling Sharon.

And how do you live with that guilt for the rest of your life?

I laid my confused head down against my forearms

and was so exhausted and traumatized that I promptly fell asleep for maybe twenty minutes. Or I suffered a stroke and passed out, who knows? I didn't want to face what came next. The music. When a cold raindrop struck my neck I opened one eye. The weather had changed. A storm front was moving in quietly from the west, no thunder, no lightning. Pockets of stars remained visible overhead as cloud fingers stretching eastward blotted some of them out. The temperature had fallen. Nothing had changed with Bubba.

Which meant that the world had changed.

I touched his shoulder again and left my hand there feeling absolutely terrified that this had happened and Bubba was gone. *How* could this have happened? Why did I throw myself out of that car? What had made the car go backward? Why couldn't Bubba evade it? What had happened? *What had happened?* Disbelief was crushing me. Horror surrounded me. I wanted to hit him to wake him up but you're not supposed to strike the dead.

I roused myself and stood up, wavering unsteadily. There wasn't a rod case to use for a cane, thus I had no equilibrium at all in the dark. After a few awkward steps I stumbled and fell, bashing my left kneecap, and strained to push upright again and gain control of my limbs. And of my head. *Concentrate*, I thought, willing myself to have balance. I *had* to walk. I had to summon help. Urgently. There was no other choice. I had wasted so much time. What was the matter with me?

Lurching at every step, I left Bubba and began to cover the five miles I must go in order to reach civilization and the authorities. "Authorities," I said aloud. Who were the authorities? I felt disoriented, in shock, befuddled, amazed, flabbergasted, panic-stricken. Who can explain by listing a bunch of adjectives? More raindrops fell at wide intervals, then they slackened and were replaced by a damp mist. I made herky-jerky progress. All around me the sagebrush glowed softly, polished by moisture and remnants of starlight.

That's when I began hallucinating and developed the eerie sensation that Bubba was traipsing along beside me. Although it was absolutely silent out I could hear him conversing with me about our slaphappy tennis matches in rainstorms and blizzards, and about the Edmonton trek we had made to see Wayne Gretzky score a goal and two assists, and about how Bubba had once needed three cushions in order to see over the steering wheel. He mentioned the book he hoped to write about his mom and dad, and also recalled some of the Big Arsenic banquets we had shared, moaning and bragging and guzzling champagne while we hugged all those laughing girls. Yuri entered the conversation, arguing about James Joyce and Tycho Brahe. "*Oh, Bubba,*" Yuri hollered soundlessly, "*you were a genius pettifogger, a truly charismatic rakehell!*"

I hate it that when people die we instantly start referring to them in the past tense.

My progress was slow and difficult. I wobbled, listing to port or to starboard from the oscillopsia. Every few minutes I lost focus, reeling, and veered off the road, pitching sideways, pinwheeling my arms to recapture balance and stop myself, ordering my body to be coordinated and take care of business. Failure was not an option. A drumbeat in my brain was: *How could that happen? What had happened? What would happen next?* And Bubba now commenced singing a song to me made famous by Waylon Jennings. It was called, "Mamas, Don't Let Your Babies Grow Up to Be Cowboys."

About halfway to the main drag I ceased thinking about anything at all, and Bubba mercifully quit bending my ears. I was in pain. Turns out I had ruptured my spleen. By then all the stars had vanished and it was raining again, this time full force. The dark silhouettes of our mountains lay before me, subdued and impersonal. Pretty soon I was drenched and more or less in agony, but I kept on walking. One foot in front of the other, you know, and with my flapping arms held out to the side for steadiness like wings.

Eight

The next spring, Yuri's widow, Sharon Adair, flew to New Mexico and we drove together up north across the state border to an elaborate memorial for Bubba at the Garden of the Gods, a majestic outdoor setting near Colorado Springs. Bubba had been a member of a golf club and resort beside the Garden, and all the stops had been pulled out for his public farewell. A stage set up beside the driving range overlooked the park's spectacular red-rock spire formations with snowcapped Pikes Peak in the background. There were microphones, loudspeakers, and hundreds of folding chairs, colorful bunting draped over nearby tree branches, an outdoor free bar, and canapé tables set up on the pro shop and family recreation center patio beside a handful of enormous grilling apparatuses just waiting to heat up the meat.

Rachel had gone to Alaska, attending the marriage of her son Maynard to a Swedish girl he had discovered in a tuna-fish canning factory near Egegik. At least five hundred mourners attended Bubba's celebration, almost none of whom I had ever met. Tawanda was there with her new beau, Ari Trappelheim, a man famous for his true adventure films shot in the Andes, on Mount Everest, and across New Guinea. Tawanda looked great. I mean, she really stood out. I was stunned. She could have been the Farah Fawcett character on *Charlie's Angels.* And Bubba's teenage daughter, Felicity Marie, had evolved into a real tall drink of water, sort of like a steamy young Tanya Tucker. I did not palaver with either of them, however, since Tawanda had always understood what Bubba was up to in my presence and I know she held resentments. I found it a jolting experience to see them both at last in the flesh. They were downright gorgeous.

There were rich entrepreneurs at the memorial, and folks from the entertainment and health spa worlds, plus ski resort big shots and a couple of professional sports team owners. Plenty of newspaper and TV personalities also. Bubba had been well-known. His family was represented by his dad, Orville, who showed up wearing a white Stetson cowboy hat, faded Wrangler jeans, and Tony Lama boots; his mom, Purcine, who looked great in a fringed western shirt with mother-of-pearl buttons, a concho belt, and a gingham skirt; and his older brother, Brian, who wore a Diamondbacks baseball hat, a brown suede jacket and green silk shirt, Levi's, and tan desert boots. During the service the old man and the brother chewed on wooden toothpicks. When Purcine Baxter rose to speak, she said, "Our boy was an angel, a bona fide saint, he took care of all of us. He never forgot his family or his roots. He called me every weekend, and he said, 'Momma, just tell me what you want and UPS will have it on your doorstep before I hang up the phone.' On every trip he made to Lubbock we went to church together. God loved Bubba, and he's singing in God's chorus now."

Brian was the only other Baxter who spoke; he did not say much. He had it all written on a piece of lined notebook paper. The oration was a kind of non sequitur about how he, Brian, could always beat Bubba at poker because Bubba talked too much and couldn't bluff, and Bubba didn't give a hoot about how much money he lost anyway because money was no object. In fact, Bubba sort of deliberately lost at poker with his brother and the old man, which was his way of giving them money without humiliating them into the bargain.

An all-girl band almost as snappy as the Dixie Chicks played country gospel tunes. You expected Jay Leno to bounce onstage and deliver a eulogy or at least crack a funny toast. Over a dozen other people spoke, and they had everyone in stitches over legendary Bubba stories, and there were a hundred rambunctious stories. Bubba had certainly made a dent. As people spoke I realized that 99.9 percent of Bubba's life had taken place far outside of my small-potatoes orbit. He had gotten *around*. Several eulogists mentioned that he was "larger than life" and "an unforgettable human being." I guess the highlight came when Bubba's old football buddy, Ricky Marples (the ex-New Orleans Saints running back), who owned a huge real-estate management firm and had sponsored the yearly Bubba Baxter Golf Tournament at the renowned Christ the Savior Country Club of Lubbock, walked up to the microphone totally snockered and dressed in a livid pink cowboy hat, a bolo tie, a fringed leather vest, maroon double-knit golf slacks, and snake-hide Lucchese boots, and said, "My friend Bubba Baxter had testicles the size of basketballs and an ego to match."

People howled and waved their hands in the air.

Nobody had asked me to speak, which was all right by yours truly. I was still way too frazzled by his death to feel I could pull it off. When the cops and EMTs finally arrived at the scene the night Bubba died, I fielded many queries from them about the accident that challenged my account of his demise. Even in its abridged version, my story was outlandish, and I knew that in some quarters a cloud hung over my head. To the authorities, on that rainy evening I had left out most of the lead-up information regarding our fishing contest. I never said "boo" about the guy firing a rifle into the gorge. Nor did I mention the crazy laps Bubba had run around his car yelling triumphantly at the top of his lungs shortly before he died. TMI. Same deal with our terrifying off-road roller coaster ride through rabbitbrush and sage, my subsequent barf-a-thon, and my deliberate self-ejection from the capsule when Bubba had rubbed in just one too many gloats. TMI squared. Fortunately, the pair of local gendarmes I summoned never drove back on the road to discover my vomit splattered all over the asphalt two miles south of the overturned SUV. By then the rain might have cleansed away the evidence, you never know.

Certainly the rain hurried their accident investigation. Our empty beer cans at the site meant I could not deny we had been drinking. Happily, neither of our blood tests indicated legal intoxication. I explained, "I neglected to close my door tightly when we departed the trailhead parking lot and it simply popped open later, catching me so unawares that I tumbled out. Bubba braked and jumped clear to rescue me and somehow the car lurched backward, killing him."

Soon after the cops and I had arrived, an ambulance came and loaded up Bubba before anyone thought to take pictures. In fact, those local officers on deck did not have a camera until a reporter showed up. By then the ambulance had already left with Bubba aboard, its destination Holy Cross Hospital in my hometown an hour south, and a wrecker was tackling the SUV. You could say that much botched police procedure had taken place. Next Thursday the front page of our weekly tabloid featured a picture of the wrecker manhandling Bubba's vehicle, yet there was no shot of yours truly. Thank God for small favors. The two cops had requested my story again in detail at their rustic station house, and they had me sign the typed statement in triplicate. Then they flagged down a state trooper named Roger Florence who drove me home.

What a strange sequence of events. I never mentioned to the police that pain in my gut. Shock, nervousness, and outright fear had momentarily quelled the hurt.

I only had a phone number for Bubba's rented Denver manor house, but the ER doctor who officially pronounced him tracked down Tawanda and gave her the news. She called the Baxter clan in Texas, and between them they arranged for a helicopter to fly Bubba to an Albuquerque funeral parlor that eventually put him on a plane to Lubbock. There, a couple of days later, Purcine, Orville, Brian, and Felicity Marie, plus a handful of neighbors, friends, and old football buddies, returned my pal to earth beside the plots he had purchased for Purcine and Orville years earlier. By then I was in the hospital fighting for my own life.

Rachel stayed with me most of that time, even sleeping on a cot in the corner. When it really hit me what had happened and why, I was paralyzed by both sorrow and guilt. Rachel listened to me, giving only a few words of condolence and advice. "Shit happens to people we love even when they're just having fun. Afterward, there's nothing to be done except learn to live with it and be grateful we're still alive. As for the grieving, it never stops. That's part of loving also."

Tawanda did not participate in the Lubbock funeral, choosing instead to concentrate on planning the splashy Colorado send-off. After the long divorce battle, she and Bubba's parents were not exactly on what you would call "speaking terms" anyway. And Tawanda and I had never talked in person. I received an invitation to the Garden of the Gods by mail, a cream-colored card with a picture on it of youthful Bubba holding a months-old Felicity Marie in his arms and feeding her a bottle. The photograph reminded me of a pietà. And I must admit that Bubba himself, just a kid awed by his brand-new daughter, looked like a cherub. An RSVP was requested and I complied, thus the organizers knew I'd be present. In fact, Bubba's editor at Harper's, Jimmy Lippencott, sent me a note, upon receiving his invitation, to say that he planned on attending the Colorado bash. Jimmy was a nice guy who'd made much hay with my blurb for *The Obnoxious Noseguard*. I would not run into him at the memorial, however, and learned later that he'd been waylaid by rehab.

If I had been urged to give a spontaneous eulogy, I suppose I would have said that Bubba was a hilarious and original American life force, as indestructible as he was outrageous, and he had been my other best friend. I might have mentioned Wayne Gretzky and the Lometa, Texas, rattlesnake roundup. For sure I would have described playing tennis through inclement weather. And of course I would have detailed our hilarious Big Arsenic adventures catching trout on the Río Grande for twenty years. That was obligatory stuff.

More to the point, however, I'd like to think I could have reminisced about the other Bubba, the quiet kid who lay in bed listening to Bill Mack's *Open Road* show from WBAP in Fort Worth-Dallas. And the boy who, when his peers called him a "dwarf," had mowed the family lawn three days a week trying to grow stronger. Perhaps I would have also recalled with compassion the adult who lay in bed at night cursing the empire he had built while wondering how to escape it in order to write a book about his mom and dad who were just ordinary, decent people. Salt of the earth. His humble and deeply respected origins.

It made sense to me that Yuri could perish before his time; he had mortality written all over him. I had never imagined that Bubba could be wiped out, though. He was too *adamant* and too *successful*, a joyous embodiment of that irresistible steam engine puffing west through the buffalo herds with bison bouncing willy-nilly off his cowcatcher, unstoppable. Then again, Bubba kept fishing with Yuri and me once a year even though our contest was the sole stupid thing he could not seem to win. This thought led abruptly to another of my revelations. Suppose Bubba had deliberately lost that contest every year so that we'd keep angling with him? Could that have been possible? Would Yuri and I have been so blind—?

Back to real life. After Ricky Marples brought down the house, there followed a sidesplitting reading from *The Obnoxious Noseguard* that had us all gasping for air. No, it wasn't an excerpt that I would have chosen. I preferred Bubba's exuberant narrator in a more contemplative mode. To wit: *Sometimes I wanted to kick butt so bad that I was ready to die trying. "Let me at 'em, coach, I know I can play!" At other times, though, I would suddenly pull up short asking myself, "Why do I wanna win so badly? What is the point if it's only a game?" And I couldn't answer that damn question. But I guessed it would haunt me for the rest of my life. God knows why I was born to be dissatisfied with anything less than everything. That ain't right but it sure is powerful.*

Next, some pompous Baptist jackanapes dressed in a tartan leisure suit appropriated the microphone and spouted a lot of scripture, then the all-girl group sang "Amazing Grace" and most of the mourners joined in. And when it ended a moving tribute happened. A handful of once athletic but now paunchy guys wearing Double T scarlet blazers and black pants pulled a contraption onto the stage called "Bangin' Bertha." It was a large cast-iron bell riveted onto a little trailer that had been dragged in a U-Haul all the way from Lubbock. The men were former members of the Texas Tech student organization called the Saddle Tramps that had been in charge of rousing school spirit. Whenever the Red Raiders scored a touchdown, the Saddle Tramps went bananas ringing the bell. And these aging Saddle Tramps now proceeded to do exactly that for almost three minutes straight, simultaneously holding their right hands raised in the *Guns up!* gesture and singing the Red Raider fight song. "You'll hit 'em high, you'll hit 'em low, you'll push the ball across the goal . . ." Many onlookers sang along shouting out the words for all the world like archangels crammed into a packed football stadium.

They surely gave Bubba his due.

When the Saddle Tramps finished their song and quit whacking the bell, a bunch of cowboy hats were tossed in the air and everybody tackled the barbecue being prepared off to the side by a dozen chefs wearing white ten-gallon sombreros with BUBBA written across the front of their crowns by glued-on crimson sequins. It was an upbeat and cheerful occasion with everyone talking at once as they stoked up on the savory grub or mingled with each other shaking hands, slapping backs, and guffawing uproariously—happy to be alive. And shortly after these festivities began I found a man standing in front of me, a man who had pushed through the noisy crowd to reach me. He stuck out his hand and introduced himself. "I'm Brian Benjamin Baxter," he said. "Bubba's older brother, the one who stayed at home."

I clasped his hand and he held onto mine gently for longer than the usual period of time.

"I'm pleased to meet you," I said.

Brian was tall and lanky, with not even half an extra pound on his frame, nearly the opposite of chunky, athletic Bubba. His hair was sandy, starting to be gray. He had calm brown eyes and a sunburned, wrinkled face like a fellow who'd ridden the Texas range all his life, although I understood that not to be the case. I believe he was fifty-three or fifty-four. And he was a man of few words.

"Thank you for coming," he said. "My mom and dad aren't comfortable meeting you here today. So I'm doing it for them. They aren't prejudiced, but they feel awkward. I hope you understand."

He paused, politely awaiting my answer.

"I understand," I said.

"My brother talked about you often." Brian kept looking at me, not in a threatening way but intensely in order to convey his sincerity. "He also read all your books. I never read any of your books. That isn't a criticism—I am not a reader. Bubba said you had more smarts than most anyone he knew, and he knew a lot of gifted people out there. He admired you for that and obviously thought the world of you. Though he had a million friends, he was particularly grateful for your friendship. He said he could *talk* with you. I want to be sure you know that."

I told him, "Thank you."

Brian let loose my hand, never smiling at me. He was not unfriendly, just shy. It had cost him an effort to get that brief speech correct and delivered to me. After nodding his head to acknowledge my thanks, he patted me on the shoulder and finished his remarks by saying, "We don't blame you for anything."

Then he turned away and weaved off through the crowd to an area beside the food tables from whence he'd come, a place where he took up his station again, checking on the milling congregation while being safely removed from it. Brian was so retiring and inconspicuous I doubt many attendees approached him to offer condolences. I kept my eye on him until I noticed that Purcine Baxter, caught in the middle of all the commotion, was tightly clutching her lovely granddaughter, Felicity Marie, both of them obviously devastated because they had lost their cherished son and beloved daddy. Believe it or not, joined with them in that embrace was Tawanda with tears streaming down her lovely cheeks. Behind the trio stood Orville gazing on uncomfortably, embarrassed by the intimate emotion being displayed in public by his wife and grandchild and daughter-in-law. Orville had removed his Stetson, which was pressed against his chest as if somebody was playing "The Star Spangled Banner."

At the boisterous center of every human maelstrom the truth will always out. And maybe that's when it hit me hardest that Bubba *was* gone, and all of us who cared for him were mourning.

· · ·

Later, as we gnawed on ribs lacquered in hickory-smoked barbecue sauce, Sharon said, "I don't know what happened to the copy of *The Obnoxious Noseguard* Bubba gave to us. I searched all over our bookcases for it after Yuri died. Yuri loved the book and he was very anal, every author arranged in alphabetical order on our shelves. But that novel wasn't among the Bs. So I checked the entire bookcase several times in case Yuri had misfiled it. I went through his desk, I rummaged in vain through everything. I don't think he loaned it out because Yuri rarely loaned his books. They were too precious. And the few he did lend, he kept the addresses and phone numbers in a file so he could call back the books if they weren't returned promptly. But *The Obnoxious Noseguard* was not in that file. It somehow disappeared. Yuri treasured the novel just as he treasured all your books, and the works by other friends, especially the signed copies. He was so proud to have friends who had been published. It was a terrible embarrassment to me that I couldn't reread Bubba's novel in Yuri's memory. I never had the courage to tell Bubba we lost it or to ask him for another signed copy. He might have been offended by our carelessness. So I walked up to the Strand and bought another copy and reread it in Yuri's honor. He had laughed so much over that story, and I laughed, too. Yuri felt he and Bubba were kindred souls, and he said Bubba could have been a great novelist if he hadn't opted to be a nattering nabob instead."

I said, "Baby, I am now going to tell you a story about your signed copy of *The Obnoxious Noseguard*."

And I finally recounted the story. I hadn't wanted to before; why rub salt in her wounds by tarnishing Bubba after Yuri's death? Let sleeping dogs lie.

When I finished, Sharon said, "I can't believe Bubba stole that book during Yuri's funeral. One year, when we were broke and I had my hysterectomy, you know what Bubba did? Uninvited? Unasked? He gave us ten thousand dollars insisting that we never pay it back. That money saved my life."

"Bubba had his little quirks," I allowed, biting my lower lip.

. . .

Sharon and I drove back from the Colorado Springs memorial on a sunny day during which the West put on a remarkable show for us. Snow patches still clung to the high mountain slopes and the grassy plains were greening up. When we rose over La Veta pass west of Walsenburg the aspen leaves were budding gold-hued green, and we had to pause at the summit for a hundred elk crossing the highway. Sharon grew melancholic because this was the type of country that Yuri had loved and had shared with me since 1971.

She had also brought with her to New Mexico the box containing half of Yuri's ashes and the pipe he had been smoking on the day he died. The other half of Yuri had gone to his mom, Barbara, who hired a plane to drop her portion into Barnegat Bay due east of Philadelphia where the child Yuri had often languished all day in a rowboat with a cane pole waiting patiently for something to bite.

So after we returned home from Bubba's memorial, Sharon and I finally geared up to distribute Yuri's ashes where his wife felt they belonged, which was down on the Río Grande.

We fashioned a picnic of baloney and swiss cheese sandwiches, Heineken beer, and, God help us, a canister of Pringles potato chips, and we cruised north with Yuri's ashes in my old Dodge D150 extended-bed pickup truck to the Big Arsenic Springs on the Wild River section of the Río Grande. Along the way we ate two sandwiches apiece, drank a couple of beers, and demolished the potato chips. At the Big Arsenic trailhead we performed what I guess you could call a sacrilege. We programmed the Nikon on a tripod for a delayed exposure, then posed together holding Yuri's box of remains between us with a rod case hard-on rising up from the box as in the olden days when our knighthoods had been in flower.

For five minutes we contemplated that dramatic rent in the earth with the gleaming trickle of water way at the bottom—our magical mystery gorge. Sharon clicked a few pictures. How could your heart not burst at such an impressive sight?

Soon we addressed the long trail that descended in a series of switchbacks to the Big Arsenic springs. A lovely day, we were lucky. For balance, I had a pair of trekking poles. We stopped to sniff the Vanilla Tree and I said, "Smell that elixir, boys." Lower down, at the fork in our path, we chose the lateral that traveled south over the sagebrush and prickly pear plateau, eventually veering deeper to the Little Arsenic Springs. Once there we began walking north along the Río Grande toward Big Arsenic. Spring runoff had the waters high and muddy. I took it easy, fighting for equilibrium every step of the way despite having the poles. Obviously, my days beside these powerful torrents were numbered.

When we arrived at the Niagara Pool where I had landed the two big rainbows on a single cast (in 1992), we stopped and took turns tossing in pinches of Yuri's ashes. Sharon choked up so thoroughly she could not talk. Being over-wrought myself, I just kept mum. As Yuri used to advise when I waxed overtly pedantic, "Cut the crap. Sometimes words ain't necessary."

I would like to report that a gigantic rainbow trout

lunged to the surface and struck the white bone fragments among Yuri's ashes with a melodramatic slashing motion that splashed us with river water, but that did not happen. The ashes disappeared lickety-split into roiling water and were gone.

We stared at the river.

Sharon said, "He was a tough little man; you could never make him cry. But nobody understood how hard he was trying to lead a decent life, to create an original work, or how gentle he could be. In private we talked for hours about philosophy, politics, the law, the natural world, environmental problems, our families, our childhoods, and all our friends. Yuri told me everything about all the books he was reading. Sure, they were lectures, yet he had amazing patience and a love of storytelling. In public his obnoxious ghetto persona was always onstage. In private we made love often and sometimes with rare delicacy. Yuri inhabited many different universes at once. He would lull me to sleep puttering along about Aristotle, or about the films of Jean Renoir, or about Sugar Ray Robinson. We all know that he never stopped talking. We fought a lot, that was his nature, mine also, but you know what? He always apologized. And he was a great cook, too. Spaghetti, linguini and clam sauce. Even just scrambled eggs and bacon for breakfast served with delicious Puerto Rican espresso coffee brewed from fresh-ground beans. I'll forever associate that aroma with Yuri."

She hugged me. We hugged each other hard and held on for a few moments. When I felt her shudder in my arms I said, "Quit feelin' sorry for yourself and take it like a man."

That caused us both to chuckle and break apart. When we did, Sharon turned her face away from me as she fetched Yuri's pipe from her pocket and was about to loft it into the river when instead she turned and abruptly presented it to me on a whim. "You keep it," she said. Her eyes were sad and mournful. "Use it on your desk for a paperweight. I want you to have it."

Yuri probably would have accused Sharon of being sappy, or he would have used a more educated word, but screw him. He had no say in the matter. If you care for somebody they can't stop you from performing rituals in their honor after they are gone. It's all sentimental blather, isn't it? However, say what you will, it's sentimental blather from the heart.

We continued hiking upstream along the riverbank, pulling ourselves together as we scrambled ineptly over, around, and between all the boulders until we reached the Big Arsenic Springs. A family at a picnic table under one of the cabanas waved us over and proclaimed they were from Carthage, Texas. A good-old boy and his good-old wife and their two bucktoothed good-old kids, a girl and a boy, maybe seven and ten respectively, blond, blue-eyed, freckled little buckaroos. They were chowing down on enough food to nourish all the starving peasants of Ethiopia for a year.

"This sure is a nifty place," the good-old lady said.

We agreed to that. Though they were friendly people, we only tarried for half a minute until starting to walk back up out of the canyon on the long winding trail, reminiscing about Yuri and Bubba and Bubba's one novel and all the years that Yuri had labored to write a piece of immortal fiction and failed, and how much Sharon had cared for him despite his irascible character—that sort of thing. It took us well over an hour to reach the rim. I was winded even worse than Sharon. My heart had undergone several tachycardia spasms that made me feel faint. I quelled them with the Valsalva maneuver.

On top, we tarried for a bit more overlooking the canyon, and I could tell Sharon was committing it to memory because she knew she would never return. It was Yuri's place and she wanted a piece of it that would be a memento of him for her. She shot a few more pictures of the deep chasm with the vein of sparkling river way at the bottom. A couple of ravens flew by. Hello, birds. And some buzzards were circling high up, my good luck charms.

We drove home and I squired Sharon to a nice meal of chile-dusted rock shrimp at Lambert's Restaurant. And the next morning I drove her to the Albuquerque airport, three hours south of my hometown.

"I'll see you around the campus," I said to Sharon after I stepped away from embracing her at the departure gate.

"Not if I see you first," she joked, with sudden tears running down her cheeks like somebody had kicked out the head gate of an irrigation ditch located right between her eyes. She took off her glasses and wiped aside the moisture, then smiled and bravely headed for the boarding tunnel.

• • •

I drove back up the highway in a reflective mood, thinking about how all things end but life goes on, and so forth.

Despite centuries of human wisdom and tortured philosophizing, nobody ever reaches a conclusion about our existence that is any more profound than that. Meanwhile, more horrors than I can recount were taking place in Afghanistan, and of course Dubya and his bloodthirsty acolytes were preparing to screw up royally in Iraq while they denied global warming, handed our exchequer over to the rich, and destroyed the US constitution. I mention this so that you'll understand I have never lived inside a bubble where only fishing and fornication were important. In fact, the Annual Big Arsenic Fishing Contest is nothing but a minuscule asterisk at the very outer edge of my personal odyssey, a tremendously unimportant footnote. Still, even insignificant blips impart an energy that is important. Not to belabor the point, but, if you wish to survive in this world, at least once a year you need to mitigate the horrors with a bit of belly laughter and meaningless yet happy fun. Otherwise, what's the purpose of being alive? Why go on? *Laugh and the world laughs with us; weep and we weep alone.*

Hence, I was not quite finished with our ignoble angling competition. Bear with me a trifle longer. My mind moves slowly, you see. I stumble on my bright ideas *after* the fact, and so now, two months after I made it home from saying good-bye to Sharon at the Albuquerque airport, I inhaled a deep breath and located a number for Bubba's ex-wife, or rather for his widow, Tawanda, and I dialed the number. Since Bubba had been dead for a spell I figured maybe the vitriol had subsided.

What I hoped for was our hand-painted wooden fish

trophy from Puerto Vallarta. I figured it should reside with me. And I wanted the copy of *The Obnoxious Noseguard* that Bubba had signed to Yuri and Sharon and then filched from them during Yuri's Manhattan memorial service. Loose ends, you know, that needed tying up.

To my surprise, Tawanda possessed both those items. That boggled my credulity. Even more astonishing, when I identified myself she began chitchatting me amicably as if we'd been next-door neighbors for years with never an acrid moment between us. She and Bubba had not yet been divorced when he was dispatched by his own SUV after the longest running divorce proceedings in America. So the former aromatherapist and her daughter, Felicity Marie, had inherited all the loot. Tawanda had sent moving vans to the Denver mini-mansion Bubba was renting when he died, and she had directed other vans to clean out his condominiums in Phoenix, Dallas, Las Vegas, and San Diego.

How the Big Arsenic fish trophy turned up was this. Bubba had it stored in the freezer compartment of his Las Vegas condo's refrigerator beside a bottle of Stolichnaya vodka and *The Obnoxious Noseguard* dedicated to Yuri and Sharon taped inside a baggie for protection. Don't ask me why, who knows? Life is a pip. One of Bubba's secretaries, name of Lindsay Friars, had been delegated to empty out that joint, boxing everything enveloped by bubble wrap and sending it to a storage facility in Denver. But Lindsay had mailed the wooden Big Arsenic fish and the book directly to Tawanda, thinking they might have meaning for Felicity Marie one day when she overcame her genetic imprinting and grew up.

Now here's another shocker. When I asked if I could have the trophy and the book back, Tawanda said, "In a New York minute, honey. I know you two dimwitted prima donnas were bosom buddies, so why not? As for the novel? I still receive royalties. And I'll be a smitch richer if they ever release that film outside of Lower Slobbovia. The actual book is fun, it's astute, and it's all true. And your friend deserves it back on her shelves."

Then I grew really bold, asking Tawanda if she would also send me one of Bubba's white Stetson cowboy hats. It had never occurred to me to salvage the headpiece he'd been wearing the day of our final contest as I had been much too busy that night schmoozing the cops, the EMTs, and the fourth estate.

"*One* of them?" She tittered gleefully. "You can have *all* of the damn things. There's a whole bin full of hats he left behind when he moved out. He was worse than Imelda Marcos."

"Just one will do the trick. I'll send you the bread for postage."

"Hang onto your money, big spender," Tawanda said. "Because of that wayward little boy's entrepreneurial genius, I'm almost a billionaire."

And then suddenly she waxed serious. "I don't know you from Adam," she professed, "but now hear this. It's no secret that for ages Bubba and I went at each other tooth and nail. Yet deep down, despite all the foofaraw, tumult, and court battles, he was *the* man of my life. And always will be. His energy was like a stallion jumping through a hoop of fire at the circus. Forget the fact that half the time he hit the flaming hoop and somersaulted his poor horse into the grandstand with a broken neck. His *attempts* were always spectacular. Put that fact in your brain and never forget it. And now good-bye and God bless, keep your powder dry, and watch out for bob wire."

. . .

A week later I received from UPS the Annual Big Arsenic fishing trophy, *The Obnoxious Noseguard* dedicated to Sharon and Yuri, and one of Bubba's white Stetson cowboy hats.

I had plans to sacrifice the trophy in a symbolic and spectacular way to honor Yuri and Bubba, yet when I actually grasped the thing in my hot little fists I acquired cold feet. It was beautiful, that fancy-painted wooden fish from Puerto Vallarta with my name written on the big tail fin in Sharpie ink seventeen times. I bet if Bubba had ever made it home after he won the contest he would have printed his name on the fish tail eight times larger than any of my multiple signatures, and he would have scrawled seven big exclamation points after his John Hancock, like this: !!!!!!! But he never made it home after that dismal afternoon, did he? There was never a full-page ad in the *New York Times*, was there? And nobody would ever know that he had come out on top, would they?

I decided I could better serve humanity and the memory of my friends by rehanging the trophy fish on my kitchen wall, and that is what I did. I'm not saying I had "won" the trophy fair and square on our last day together, I was merely displaying it in honor of Yuri and Bubba and to remember all the good times we shared. In my heart I knew Bubba was the "champ," and thank goodness for that. Nobody wants an ill-begotten tourist geegaw hanging around their neck like an albatross. Then again, no harm was done by featuring the trophy on my wall. And, legally, it probably should have been retired after our eighteenth year because of the mercy rule. They do that in Little League, don't they?

Look on my fish, ye mighty, and despair.

Next, I attached a shoelace chinstrap to Bubba's Stetson and hung the hat off a nail driven into my adobe wall right beside the wooden icon from Puerto Vallarta. They looked good together. I hooked a little brown fly and a little black fly onto the front brim of the Stetson to spruce it up and admired the effect. Presto! I had myself a bonny altar on the wall. It made me feel . . . sad . . . and yet grateful for all the fun we'd had . . . and also, I must admit, maybe just a tad squeamish.

The following day I sent Sharon the copy of *The Obnoxious Noseguard* that Bubba had purloined during Yuri's memorial. Sharon called me when she received it, extravagantly grateful.

"You're an ace," she said. "Thank you, thank you."

"Don't thank me, Sharon, thank Bubba Baxter. On top of everything else, he once wrote a really good book."

• • •

And then you know what I did? I removed from my self-defrosting refrigerator the frozen cutbow that Bubba had caught on our last day fishing together, unwrapped the handsome specimen, and thawed it slowly on a platter beside my kitchen stove. Despite the year-long time lapse the corpse had suffered no freezer burn. The way I prepare trout is real basic. As Richard Nixon once said, "I am not a cook." I melt butter in the frying pan, salt it a little, then slide in the fish. I have an instinct for how long I should fire up each side. When I remove the trout I squeeze on a few drops of juice from a fresh lemon slice, lift the tail, and with my fork I nudge down each strip of flesh off the bones and vertebra and commence nibbling away.

On this occasion, witnessed by nobody, I lit my only candle and poured myself a glass of eight-dollar cabernet, which is about my speed. Anything fancier is wasted on my hillbilly taste buds. You can't impress me with a Châteauneuf-du-Pape. I don't mind admitting that I'm a Philistine. Maybe not born and bred, but over the years I have studiously cultivated a working-class lack of wine sophistication so that, proudly, I can say, "I am *not* an oenophile."

Yuri taught me that word.

It was a fine trout and later the skeleton disappeared into my garbage dumpster and was hauled away by a city truck. That night I had a dream about my own funeral. It was a vivid dream and immediately I scribbled it as best I could remember on a yellow legal pad I've always kept (along with a flashlight) beside my bed so that I can write stuff down when I wake up abruptly in the dark.

Yuri and Bubba were the lone pallbearers carrying my coffin through sagebrush on the wide mesa west of town. Nobody lived out there, hence zero houses stood around. Just sagebrush, not a single tree, and tall mountains ten miles east on the other side of the Río Grande gorge. Bubba carried the coffin by a brass handle in front, and Yuri held onto a brass handle in back. It was a simple pine box that I gather had been manufactured by both of them together. The sunshine was brutal.

They lugged my coffin over to the edge of the gorge and set it on the ground. You could see the river down there, snaking along far below between the cliff walls. Bubba wiped his brow with a red-checked neckerchief then handed it to Yuri, who patted his forehead and returned the bandana to Bubba. The casket had no lid on it and I lay supine in there naked as a jaybird except for one of my novels opened facedown over my crotch for propriety's sake like a miniature splayed-out tent. My eyes were closed and I seemed peaceful. My hands had been folded serenely across my belly by the attendants. I had very recently died and was not embalmed.

Bubba said, "It's a pity he died so young. There's a lot more trout in that river he could have caught. He had a knack with a fly rod that I admired."

Yuri gave Bubba one of his patented inner-city gangster glowers. "What are you mumbling about? He was the clumsiest son of a bitch I ever knew, but you're right—he could catch trout. I don't believe he pulled them from the river, however. I bet he shit fish on demand, then shoveled them out of his britches into the creel. He wrote books the same way."

Bubba protested, "I don't think you should denigrate his talents. He might not have been a top-notch angler or novelist, yet his energetic mediocrity had an admirable panache."

Yuri borrowed the neckerchief again and blew his nose into it, balled it up, took five steps backward, did a quick feint to the left, then to the right, pretended to dribble, stopped, and lofted a basketball jump shot that landed the clotted piece of cloth right on top of me in the pine box.

"Let's get on with the show," he said.

Crouching behind the coffin, Yuri and Bubba pushed as if my remains were held captive inside a stalled automobile. The box slid across the sand, gramma grass, pebbles, and a few baby horned toads right beyond the cliff edge and into the gorge. My pals straightened up, dusting off their hands— good riddance. Except the casket did not tumble end over end down the boulder-strewn slopes splintering apart as my body got tossed free and was shredded by prickly pear and cholla cacti on the way to hellfire and damnation. Instead, my coffin sailed off the edge of the precipice and out over the deep gorge like a rowboat on a quiet lake and began floating southward as smooth as silk on warm air currents rising above the river. I didn't fall at all. In fact, I could just as well have been reclining on an air mattress atop the calm water of a swimming pool.

For some reason, even though I lay inside the container with my eyes closed, I was able to observe violet-green swallows as they drifted in slow motion overhead like delicate origami birds. And I could also see backward to where Bubba and Yuri stood at the cliff edge waving good-bye.

"So long," they cried in unison. "It's been good to know you!"

Epilogue

Twelve more months went by. I felt like an orphan, abandoned and all alone. I had a longing for my buffoonish friends, for the immature bantering that had driven our yearly expeditions up the river between the Little and the Big Arsenic Springs. In my daydreams I often heard Yuri's scornful commentary: "Your insults are like a gentle caress." Yes they were, and I yearned for those insults again. Too bad there was nobody else in my life like Yuri and Bubba willing to be so brazenly asinine. Henceforth, I guess I was doomed to be grown-up.

Sometimes I lay in bed running Bubba's demise over and over again in my head. And of course it never came out any different. You can't rewind the film once it's developed and shoot a different movie. I kept jerking open that SUV door and tumbling out into the sagebrush and cactus plants. "I'm a murderer," I whispered to Rachel when she appeared to be fast asleep. "How could I do a thing like that to my friend?"

She opened one eye and pressed a finger against my lips, shushing me with, "You can't spend the rest of your life saying 'I'm sorry.'"

"How can I make amends?" I asked her.

"It's over, darlin'. Life goes on for the rest of us."

"Who will forgive me?" I insisted.

"Look in the mirror," she said.

However, when things aren't right you can't ignore them for too long. In my latter years I have become a terrible procrastinator, yet sooner or later I *do* get cracking with what has to be done. And what happened is that I abruptly decommissioned the "bonny altar" on my kitchen wall, and drove once more up the highway to the Wild River section of the Río Grande on a lovely early autumn afternoon with my fishing rod in tow and Rachel Ivory seated beside me.

She and I had known each other now, and been involved off and on, for over eighteen years. As strange as this may seem, we had become serious friends and our argumentative personalities lacked fire anymore. We had no plans to remarry again, yet I believed we'd remain united for the duration. My hair was turning gray and so was Rachel's. True enough, every now and then the old antagonizing passions reappeared. Rachel explained to me that love and hate derive from the same emotional reservoir; anger and sexual ecstasy are twin outbursts of the identical arousal mechanisms. We copulate and kill each other for almost the same reasons. And it never pays to grow smug in any human relationship—that is the secret of endurance.

I'm sure the initial rough years of the twenty-first century had something to do with it, nudging us to inhabit a more tempered friendship rather than our former intoxicating erotic altercations. *Love is not a hundred yard dash, it's a marathon.*

My older daughter, Stephanie, perceived it this way: "You're like a decrepit old elk pushed out to the edge of the herd, Dad. However, the nearby salivating wolves can't take you down quite yet." Stephanie's kids, Callie, Sally, and Roger were fanatical little hip-hop dancers and Stephanie had recently published her first (and soon-to-be quite popular) novel about a one-legged private detective from Budapest who hunted down former Nazis in Costa Rica. Like father, like daughter. Her younger sister, Naomi, said, "I like the new you, Pop, and it's sweet that your nose is always dripping." Naomi had already divorced the Los Alamos physicist and become a midwife delivering babies out on the Navajo reservation at Chinle. The girls' mother, Gretchen, was a successful potter who traveled around America in a large RV selling her handcrafted wares at ceramic conventions. On my most recent birthday she had mailed me a clay coffee mug with a leaping trout for its handle.

I walked down to the Little Arsenic Springs wearing Bubba's white Stetson cowboy hat, which was a fraction large but that was to be expected. Those two flies were still hooked onto the front brim. Rachel proceeded ahead of me the way she did when we hiked anywhere, a point of order with her and for decades I had deferred to it. She carried the two sections of my fly rod while I kept myself steady with the trekking poles. The sky was robin's-egg blue, framing a few puffy white clouds brightened by warm autumn sunshine.

"Just another day in Paradise," I said.

"My sentiments exactly," Rachel answered.

Rigging up where Yuri, Bubba, and I had always started

our competition, I began fishing north along the rugged stretch leading eventually to the Big Arsenic Springs. Between casts I shoved the butt end of my rod, which was pointed straight up, into the left side of my knapsack, and used the trekking poles to reach the next hole. Slow going, but we were not in a hurry. No pressure. How nice to be on the river in that mood, relaxed, almost like Yuri regarding the rushing waters while he smoked his pipe. I meant to enjoy every moment of the afternoon.

Although no breeze stirred, the day was not uncomfortably hot or placid. Rachel followed on the boulders above me, moving across the rock tops with a graceful coordination that I envied. Her body was in good shape and strong. Her hair drawn back in a ponytail gave her an almost teenage aura. After all these years she still exuded a golden light. Observing her made me cheerful and it caused a catch in my throat.

The river was running a trifle murky from recent rain showers, yet the fish were biting. Rachel and I refrained from talking. She accompanied me quietly, enjoying the river and the pleasant weather, stopping when I paused to cast. I caught a small brown trout and played it to shore and released it into a foamy back eddy. "Have a good life, little fella." Shoreline grasses had a faint yellow gleam, and poison ivy leaves were turning crimson. The wild milkweed and apache plume displayed silky seed tufts. Among the boulders you could smell pine needles and nature seemed glad to be so vibrant. I felt happy myself, survivors always do.

I paused often to contemplate the water. Having all the time in the world for reflection, I naturally indulged myself.

I had been fishing the little streams and thirty-six miles of this river since I moved out west in 1970. I started when I was thirty and now I was sixty-three. I knew most of the trails on the eastern and the western sides of the gorge, although some had been more my favorites than others. Those paths down to the river had names like Rattlesnake, Sheep Corral, Suicide Slide, Caballo, Gutiérrez, Francisco Antonio, and Hole-in-the-Rock. Others were called Miner's Trail, Ox Trail, Cedar Springs, Bear Crossing, Rope Trail. In my county probably not ten people were left who had once descended those steep bajadas to fly-fish for trout on the dramatic Río Grande. Old-timers die; people forget; things change.

"I *own* the Río Grande," I whispered. "You don't believe me? Just look at its number tattooed upon my wrist."

On a resplendent September afternoon Rachel and I were surrounded by immense, grandiose terrain—name an inflated adjective. Boulders and noisy white water, high canyon walls, juniper and ponderosa trees. Though I did not have the balance or the bravery to hop across the river on the stones anymore, I could deal. After all, I was still *here*. I was tall, I was skinny, I wore glasses . . . and I alone had lived to tell this tale.

It's a blue blood affectation.

Rachel moved upriver along the boulders above me like my shadow, like my other self, like my partner. We had grown tolerant and compliant together after crossing a dozen mysterious Rubicons along the way. There aren't easy answers to the riddles of devotion, or maybe there are no permanent answers at all. You don't want to question things and jinx them. Our love was unconditional *and* ambiguous.

I spotted raccoon tracks on a small sandbar, and then a killdeer ran along the shore in front of us. Tiny midges were floating around. Also large blue darner dragonflies. I had an interesting scuffle with a chunky rainbow that I breathed carefully before scootching it back into the current. In short, no fish would die that day. As a matter of fact, I have not killed a trout on the Río Grande or on any other stream since Bubba Baxter caught his infamous cutbow in the nineteenth year of our Annual Big Arsenic contest.

I am not a fisherman anymore.

When we reached the area where Bubba had beached his winning trout while I crouched behind a stone because some doofus was firing rifle bullets into the gorge, I quit casting and parked myself on a modest rock. Rachel came down and sat on a boulder next to me. I surveyed all around us. It was like revisiting Pearl Harbor or Waterloo. Large basalt obstructions littered the river, and talus slides rose on the opposite shore, and, higher, sheer cliff walls went straight to the rim. About two-thirds of the way up the western canyon wall I spotted a large V-shaped white stain under a ledge where hawks, or owls, or maybe eagles had their aerie. Above the canyon rim was a strip of azure sky with white clouds hanging there very peaceful and benign.

The time had come to honor my departed comrades properly.

Dropping to earth, I took off Bubba's Stetson, kissed the crown, and set the hat upside down on the sand. "You're the champ, Bubba," is what I said out loud so he could hear me

. . . and then I repeated those words. From my heart and with no holds barred, I assure you.

After that, I removed Yuri's pipe from my pocket and put it inside Bubba's hat. Then I lifted the inverted hat and placed it carefully in the river, which immediately carried it off.

Next, I unzipped my knapsack and removed the Big Arsenic wooden fish trophy, and, giving myself no time for second thoughts, I flung it after Bubba's hat with Yuri's pipe inside. The trophy landed with a splash, spun around in a circle, and began chasing after the Stetson. Ultimately, those talismans did not belong to me, or to Yuri, or to Bubba, they belonged to the Río Grande.

Stiffly, I climbed onto Rachel's perch and sat beside her with my left hand on her thigh. She settled her right hand over mine.

The hat floating upside down on the water was swept away like our own lives are being swept away even as I write. It's a powerful current that carries us all downstream to a mythical Gulf of Mexico, and it is a long and bumpy journey to get there, but the time goes by really fast if you're having fun. If you're not having fun, that's tough, but at least you shouldn't bitch about it. "Quit feelin' sorry for yourself and take it like a man."

They had been champs, Bubba and Yuri, both of them, and I mourn them still. Comes many an evening when I pour two ounces of Wild Turkey upon a cube of ice in my glass for old time's sake and drop in a maraschino cherry. Then I lean back, closing my eyes, and remember how we looked at the Big Arsenic trailhead with our rod-case erections raised on high and our wild grins shining forth. There is a line in Bubba's novel that goes like so: *When you come right down to it, friendship is way more important than money, pussy, or a leather bag full of ambition.* And the opening riff of Yuri's second unpublished masterpiece contains this sentence: *I once had two eccentric confederates with whom I dallied away the carnival days of my youth ecstatically performing adolescent chicaneries.*

Amen.

I followed Bubba's hat with my eyes for about twenty seconds. It never got swamped or tipped over. The wooden fish trophy caught up to it and for a brief instant they raced side by side. The Stetson swirled around some rocks, dived over a little falls, and slowed down briefly in a wider channel, growing tiny, becoming a bright speck that disappeared where the river itself seemed to vanish into a garden of enormous smooth boulders made of black basalt. Then the hat and the wooden fish were consumed, as we all shall be one day, by eternity.

"*Ne frusta vixisse videar,*" I said.

Rachel squeezed my hand.

And the Annual Big Arsenic Fishing Contest was over, except for the memories.